BREAKING ALL THE RULES

Samantha Baca

Contents

<u>One</u>
Eva
Two Weeks Ago

"It's so crowded and noisy in here," I whined as I plopped down on the leather padded barstool and pulled at my skirt that kept riding higher up my thigh. I regretted very few things in life, but tonight was filled with them. For example, letting my best friend, Brittany, and my two younger sisters convince me to get dressed up and come out with them to a packed bar in Manhattan on a Monday night. This wasn't my type of scene. I would much rather be at home, comfortable in my sweats, watching reruns of Jeopardy.

"It's barely even busy," Brittany said with a laugh. "Try coming here on the weekend—you can't even hear yourself think, let alone move."

"So, why are we here again?" I looked around the room as I drummed my hands on my thighs anxiously under the high-top table. I had no idea what I was looking for, but something deep down told me that it was my excuse to get the hell out of there—or at least I hoped it did.

"We're here because you've been cooped up and wallowing by yourself in that tiny apartment of yours for six months, and you need some damn fun in your life," my middle sister, Gabi, replied, lifting the shot glass the waiter had just set in front of her. I glanced down at mine as I felt their judgmental gazes, likely expecting me to be boring and predictable.

Fuck it.

I lifted the glass, pulled my shoulders back, and took a deep breath in. She was right. I had been wallowing for six months, but she seemed to forget that it wasn't because I was boring and lonely. It was after my *fiancé* left me for another woman. And I wouldn't technically call it *wallowing*. It was more that I was trying to find who I was *without* Jeremy, and it was taking a little longer than I cared to admit. How I had allowed myself to get so lost while I was with him was beyond me.

Ending our relationship wasn't something that I saw coming. Just like I hadn't expected to catch him getting a blow job under his desk one night when I took him dinner because I felt bad that he was working late. But you live, you learn, and you move on for the most part. The moving on portion was still a little complicated for me because even though I didn't love Jeremy anymore, I had spent a good portion of my life trying to be what I thought he wanted, only to find out he wanted something else. The bastard stole every tiny ounce of happiness I had, along with my toaster. *For my own good, my ass...*

"Cheers," I said with as much enthusiasm as I could muster. My cheeks hurt from the fake smile I was forcing.

I tilted my head back and opened my mouth, allowing the liquid to burn my throat on its way down. There was no way in hell that I was reaching for my Diet Coke as a chaser— even if I needed it. If they wanted to see wild and crazy Eva, they were going to get wild and crazy Eva. I shook my head excitedly like I was having the time of my life before setting the empty shot glass down on the table.

I knew they were watching because I could feel their eyes on me. But those weren't the only ones. I could feel the heat from across the room as his gaze bore into me before I found him. The room was dimly lit, so it was hard to see the full details of the man sitting at a private table in the VIP area. However, from what I *could* see, he was drop-dead gorgeous.

The women around him desperately tried to get his attention as they paraded in front of him in their micro-dresses, but he didn't seem to notice as he kept his eyes on me. His tall frame leaned back against a leather couch as he slowly lifted his glass of what I assumed was whiskey to his lips. His dark hair looked like he had been freshly fucked as it stood slightly mussed on his head, my fingers itching to run through it.

I didn't even know this man, yet he had fire spreading through my veins just from the way he continued to stare at me. It was almost as if he was a predator and I was his prey.

When he lowered his glass, a designer watch slid down his wrist, catching in the lights above him. An equally attractive man sitting next to him leaned in to tell him something. He nodded subtly and looked around, his eyes finding me easily again as the crowd of people between us started to thicken in the packed nightclub.

He didn't strike me as the kind of man who frequented these sorts of establishments, but then again, with the smoking hot smolder he had going on, I couldn't see why he wouldn't. He could literally have any woman in the room if he wanted—including me.

"I knew it. Just one night out with us was all she needed," Lucy, my baby sister, sang as she reached over and patted me on the back with a smile.

As much as she wanted to stay true to her wild ways, her touch was more of a mother than a party girl with those days long past her. I felt a pang in my chest when I thought about how big her fight was going to be with her husband when she got home tonight. While I personally didn't love going out for a girl's night that often, Lucy wasn't usually allowed to.

"I wouldn't get too excited over that," Gabi snorted. "She's only done one shot and looks like a caged animal, ready to bolt the second she can. Look at the way she's intently scoping out the room, her eyes darting back and forth as if she's desperate to find an exit."

I raised an eyebrow and locked eyes with her. I recognized the unspoken challenge she was issuing. The problem was that I didn't know if I actually wanted to accept it. Suddenly, her features softened as if she were pitying me, and my mind was made. I didn't want or *need* anyone's pity.

The waiter returned a few minutes later with the second round of shots that Gabi had immediately requested after he dropped off the first round. Once they were on the table, I reached over and swiped Gabi's from her. In one swift movement, I downed her shot and mine, then slammed the empty glasses on the table as I raised an eyebrow at her.

Tequila was never my drink of choice, mainly because it always resulted in a terrible headache the next day. But it was worth it if it meant that I was headed in the right direction of getting my family to stop thinking that I was some broken woman who didn't know how to have fun anymore. Sure, I was approaching forty, but it wasn't like I was some crazy cat woman who relied on them to keep me company on my lonely nights. I had fun; it was usually just confined to the comfort of my apartment, and it ended before nine o'clock.

I could hear Brittany hootin' and hollerin' beside me, cheering as she pointed at Gabi and laughed at how I stole her drink. She definitely drew attention to our table, but there was one person who was taking even more interest than anyone else. I watched as a cocky grin spread across his face before he set his glass down on the table in front of him and stood up. He adjusted his tie and jacket before scooting out between tables and giving a slight nod to the security guard standing at the roped entrance of the VIP section. A casual glance over his shoulder was the last thing I noticed before I slid off my barstool and pulled down my skirt.

Three shots of tequila in under fifteen minutes would give anyone the same confidence as a two-year-old dancing to their favorite song. I looked down at my chest, thankful that I had given in and borrowed Brittany's tank top that showed off my cleavage in a way that screamed sexy, not slutty. Although, the tight black skirt with a slit up to my thigh and six-inch stiletto heels didn't necessarily say *good girl* either.

I wiggled my fingers next to my thighs, trying to dispel some of the energy that was coursing through me. It wasn't like I was planning to do anything—was I?

Just because I jumped off my barstool quicker than a clown at a rodeo didn't mean I was expecting anything to happen as I followed him through the pool of bodies on the way to the bathroom. Maybe I just really needed to pee after consuming so much alcohol in such a short time.

My nerves finally started to calm down as I tried to rationalize that I wasn't stalking him; I was just answering nature's call. But when I rounded the corner to the hallway where the bathrooms were and plowed right into him, my body quickly convinced me that all of that was bullshit. I was ready to answer another type of call…

His hand gently wrapped around my waist, steadying me as I stumbled and lost my balance.

"You okay?" he asked, his voice low and gruff, sending a memo directly to my vagina that this sound would be added to my sexy playlist of things I thought about when I was by myself.

"Yeah," I stammered, refusing to look up and meet the heated gaze that was on me. "Sorry. I didn't see you there."

"Well, that's a shame. And here I thought you must have seen me since you followed me to the bathroom."

Against my better judgment, I decided to look up slowly and found dark brown eyes fixated on me. That same cocky smile I had seen not too long ago flashed across his face, showing off the perfect dimples in his cheeks. He pulled his bottom lip in between his teeth before popping it free, the fullness of it making me want to lean in and bite it.

"I wasn't following you," I said quietly, trying to find that tequila-laced confidence that I had only a few minutes ago.

"You sure about that?" He tilted his head to look at me, his hand still warm against my lower back. If he moved it down just slightly, it would be firmly planted on my ass. As if reading my thoughts, he raised his eyebrows and lowered his hand. I could feel the heat radiating off of my body as it begged for more.

"Yeah, I was just heading to the bathroom myself."

"Well, then, I won't keep you." He slowly stepped away, lowering his hand from my body as his fingers brushed across my ass, sending shivers up my spine.

Perhaps it was the tequila running through my veins or the lack of sex, but something changed deep inside, forcing me to act on impulse. I grabbed his hand, pulling him into me as I wrapped my arms around his neck and pressed my lips against his. His lips immediately parted as his tongue licked across my lips, begging for entrance.

Strong hands wrapped around my waist, then dipped down and brushed against my ass as he walked us back against the wall so we were out of the way of those walking past us. I heard a few girls whispering about how hot he was but ignored the comments about why he would choose someone like me. Their opinions didn't matter right now. All that mattered was the hard bulge that was pressed against my thigh as his mouth devoured mine.

Suddenly, he broke the kiss and pulled away, running a hand down the scruff that dotted his jawline.

"Come with me," he growled, taking me by the hand and leading me down the hallway into a private area marked with employee-only signs.

"I don't think we're supposed to be back here," I whispered, looking around to make sure no one was going to catch us.

"It's fine," he responded quickly before pulling me into a linen closet and closing the door behind us.

It was too dark to see anything, but within a few seconds, he turned on the flashlight on his phone before setting it on the shelf beside us. He reached over and grabbed me, pulling me back into his arms as his mouth trailed kisses down my neck.

I could feel the aching between my thighs. The wetness that was already starting to pool against the thin fabric of my black lace thong. My chest heaved as he kissed me, lowering his mouth to my breasts as his hands reached up and cupped them.

"Are you sure you want to do this?" he asked, his breath tickling my skin.

"Yes," I moaned, leaning in to get closer to him as he licked along the lace of my bra before pulling the cup down with his teeth and exposing a pebbled nipple. His lips immediately found it, pulling it in and sucking hard as a wave of pleasure spread over me.

"Say it. I need to make sure we're on the same page with what we are doing here."

"I want you to fuck me."

"Turn around," he growled, pulling away from me to give me space to do so.

I did as he asked, bracing myself against the shelf in front of me. It didn't look the sturdiest, but my options were limited in the small linen closet.

My heart raced through my chest so loudly that I barely heard the sound of him unzipping his pants and tearing the foil on the condom wrapper. He pushed my skirt further up my thighs, the chill in the air nipping at my ass that was fully exposed and in plain sight for him now.

"Fuck, you have a nice ass. I wish we had more time so I could truly enjoy it."

"Thank you," I replied coyly over my shoulder as I felt his cock brush against my ass.

I held on tight to the shelf as I spread my legs as far as I could without losing my balance as his fingers edged under my thong and slid inside of me. I gasped at the welcomed intrusion, pleased with how wet and ready I was for him. Then he slid another finger inside and I thought I was going to come right then and there. I let my head roll back, resting against his chest as I enjoyed the feel of his slightly rough hands on my body.

"You're so fucking wet," he growled against my ear as his fingers pumped faster and harder. "I bet you taste delicious, don't you?"

I nodded, unable to respond because any functional brain cells I had at this point were focused on my clit, which he was now rubbing with his thumb. Before I was ready for him to stop, he pulled his hand away and stuck his fingers in his mouth, sucking them before making a popping sound when he pulled them free.

"I knew it. Delicious," he said with a low chuckle. "Now I want to feel how good that pussy feels wrapped around me. You think you're ready for this big cock?"

I nodded again. I was full-on panting at this point, on the verge of coming undone in a linen closet. There was no way I was in any shape to speak actual words to him. Firm hands gripped my hips, holding me in place as he lined his cock up at my entrance and slowly pushed inside.

"Ahhhh," I cried out, intense pleasure threatening to overcome my body any second now. He was beyond well endowed. He was downright huge. My pussy tightened around him, forcing him to stop for a second so I could get used to his size. I tried to spread my legs further so he could go deeper, but the sound of fabric tearing as I felt the slit on my thigh spread forced me to stop. There was no way I was going to be able to walk out of here and pretend nothing happened if I had a slit all the way up to my vagina.

I tried to stifle the moans of pleasure that were desperate to come out, knowing that we couldn't risk getting caught. His fingers reached down between my legs again, rubbing my clit as he pumped harder, fucking me perfectly from behind. I could feel the pressure building as he went faster, his fingers working in perfect time with his cock.

I couldn't take it anymore as I tilted my head back and groaned, feeling my pussy pulse against his fingers and cock as my orgasm ripped through me. He slowly removed his fingers, bringing them up for me to taste myself before he grabbed my hips tighter and slammed into me repeatedly until he found his own release.

We stayed there for a few minutes, leaning against each other as our breathing started to return to normal. As good as I felt, I knew that I couldn't turn around and look at him the way I wanted to. That would be far too intimate for what this really was. But we also couldn't stay in the linen closet forever either.

I stepped away from him after he slowly pulled out and took a moment to fix my skirt—or what was left of it. I had no idea how bad the damage was since it was still dark in here, but it was worth it. He worked quietly behind me as he situated himself. Luckily, we were right by the bathrooms so I could sneak in and fix whatever I needed to so no one knew what we had just done.

"You alright?" he asked, his voice more relaxed than it was earlier.

"Yeah," I said, not sure if I was lying. "Great."

Okay, so that part wasn't a lie. I did feel great. Better than I had in a long time, likely because I just had the best sex of my life with some random stranger in a linen closet.

But I didn't have time to stop and dwell on that because it was only a matter of minutes before my sisters and Brittany came looking for me, and this was something I *didn't* want to have to explain.

"After you," he said softly, opening the door and stepping to the side to let me through.

I smiled nervously before stepping out and looking around to see if anyone had seen us.

Thankfully, the coast was clear. I heard him walk out behind me and close the door. Suddenly, it was awkward, and I had no idea what to say. It wasn't like I knew him. Hell, we didn't even bother to ask each other's names. But did that even matter? It wasn't like we would ever see each other again. One night of fun was all that this was.

We walked in silence down the empty hallway, back

toward the bar, where the noise was getting louder the closer we got. Right as we reached the turn for the bathrooms, I was about to excuse myself when a burly man with a thick beard rounded the corner and startled me.

"There you are!" His voice boomed around us. "I was looking all over for you. Brent wants to discuss what the profit-sharing will look like before we move any further."

I was thankful for the distraction when the guy wouldn't shut up long enough for him to get a word in, which meant I was off the hook for some weird goodbye with him. They continued walking back to the club while I made a quick pit stop in the ladies' room.

Soft music floated overhead from the speakers in the corner, making it feel more peaceful than the club really was. I leaned over the sink and took a glance in the mirror, my eyes widening when I saw a red mark on my neck from where he had been kissing me. My fingers trailed over it, a fresh reminder of what I had just done. In a way, I was officially branded, just like in the Scarlet Letter.

I heard a toilet flush and snapped back to reality, pretending to fix my hair as the stall door opened and the sound of high heels approached where I was standing at the counter.

"There you are. We thought you left," Brittany said, taking a spot next to me at the sink. She eyed me curiously before turning on the water to wash her hands. I knew that look. I *hated* that look. It was the one that she had every time she could sense there was juicy gossip to share.

"Nope, just went to the bathroom," I lied as I lifted my finger to wipe off some of the lipstick that was smeared along my bottom lip. I had hoped she hadn't caught it, but the look on her face confirmed she had.

"Really?" She raised an eyebrow and stared at me in the mirror. "That's the lame-ass lie you're going with?"

"What?" I raised my hands beside me. "I'm in the bathroom. You're in the bathroom. Why is that so hard to believe?"

She let out a long, slow, *overly dramatic* breath before turning to grab a paper towel from the dispenser on the wall. I felt my anxiety starting to build again as she took her time drying her hands, making me wait for her to say something. I knew that she knew something had happened, but the tension kept building the longer she waited to confirm it.

"Because, Eva, no one was in the bathroom when I came in. I know that for a fact because I checked every single stall looking for you."

Fuck. I swallowed hard, my throat suddenly dry and scratchy.

"I got lost on my way," I shrugged. My face flushed with embarrassment as heat flamed across it all the way to my ears.

"You got lost?"

I nodded and shrugged again. My fingers trembled slightly as I pushed a strand of hair back behind my ear, pretending to fix my hair to avoid the look I was getting.

"So, where were you?" she prodded, tapping her foot next to me as she leaned back against the counter, now facing me.

"I was just walking around, looking for the bathrooms," I lied, hearing the change in my voice at the same time she picked up on it. It only ever got that high when I was lying.

"Then what happened to your skirt? The slit is ripped." She pointed down to the tear that was so high that I was worried my vagina was going to pop out at any moment and greet the people of Manhattan.

"I tripped."

The temperature rose around me as the air grew thick with the lies I was spurting out.

"On a dick?"

"Brittany!" I shrieked. My hands flew up, trying to cover my face so she couldn't see the truth about it. But it was pointless. Her face lit up when she finally noticed the crimson flush across my chest, neck, and face.

"I want ALL. OF. THE. DETAILS!" she squealed excitedly.

"I'm not going to tell you what happened!"

"You just did," she said with a shrug. "Your body language gives you away every time. And this time, it just so happens to include too many details for you to skimp over. So, start talking."

She wrapped her arm in mine, leading me out of the bathroom. We talked quickly as we made our way back to the table. I wasn't ready to give my sisters the details of what had just happened, especially since I was still processing it. But overall, I guess they were right about one thing: a night out on the town wasn't so bad after all.

Two
Eva

I rubbed my hands together anxiously, trying to fight the nerves of first-day jitters. It wasn't the first time that I had started a new job, but it was the first time that I had been offered a position as a lawyer at a prestigious corporate law firm in Manhattan. Roberts and Associates was literally at the top of my dream board of businesses that I wanted to work for. Aside from their highly competitive wages and ridiculous sign-on package, they also worked with some of the most elite clients in New York. If you wanted to move up the ladder in this business, this was the place to do it.

I glanced in the mirrored walls that lined the elevator, making sure I still looked okay. I must've looked at myself a hundred times before I left my apartment and hopped on the train, worried that somehow, I would show up for my first day looking completely unprepared. I had to remind myself that as long as I was confident and strong on the outside, it didn't matter if I was a complete train wreck on the inside.

The bell dinged as the doors spread apart, opening to a pristine white marbled floor that extended the entire length of the room. I stepped off the elevator and walked to the reception desk that sat comfortably beneath the *Roberts and Associates* sign mounted to the wall above it. I had been to the building for my interview; however, it was in a separate location on the twenty-first floor.

All of the offices, including mine, consumed the *entire* twenty-second floor. I had even heard rumors that some of the partners had their own private elevators and personal gyms in their offices. You could practically live here with all the amenities that they provided, which made me wonder if that was part of the job. Maybe they made it seem like these were all perks when, in reality, it was just to give you what you needed since you would practically live there.

I stood in front of the vacant desk and waited, tugging nervously at the hem of my skirt while I tried to push the negative thoughts out of my head. I hadn't seen a bell to ring to notify anyone that I was there, but then again, this wasn't any ordinary office. They probably had cameras and sensors that alerted them when someone was there. I looked up and scanned the walls, searching for evidence of one when the door to my right opened, and a pretty blonde woman walked out. She smiled politely as she approached, as if she already knew who I was and what I was doing there.

"Hi, I'm Eva," I started, extending my hand to her. She pulled her lips into a fake smile and tilted her head to the side.

"Yes, Ms. Sanchez, we're so excited to have you start today. Please come with me."

She turned on her heel and walked to the door where she had come from, holding it open. I followed her inside, taking in the open, airy hallway lined with framed awards on the cream-colored walls. The beautiful, marbled floor continued down the hallway, adding a touch of elegance. We walked around the corner and stopped in front of a glass door that opened into a large conference room with floor-to-ceiling glass walls.

"The others will be here soon," Regina, the Director

of Human Resources, said as she smiled when I stepped into the conference room. She had been so nice when I met her during my interview, so it was nice having a friendly face to start my first day.

I was thankful that no one else was here for the meeting yet since my nerves were already out of control. Walking into a room of unfamiliar faces waiting for me might have sent me over the edge.

She gave me another warm smile and asked that I take a seat at the table, assuring me that we would get started soon. I chose a spot toward the back of the room, furthest away from where she was standing to avoid drawing attention to myself during the meeting. Soon, the room had filled and almost all of the seats were taken, except for the one right beside me at the end of the table.

Regina looked around and smiled, reminding me of a schoolteacher who was taking mental notes of no-show and tardy students. Her eyes landed on the empty seat next to me before she subtly shook her head and got started. I tried to keep myself focused on the meeting and the updates she was discussing regarding changes in the employee handbook.

It wasn't the most exciting conversation, though I couldn't imagine that proper work attire was ever considered a thrilling conversation amongst the group of board members and senior lawyers who were in the room. The older women scoffed at the idea of a skirt that was shorter than six inches above the knee, making me reach down and pull at mine.

As Regina continued to discuss the changes that were being made, I heard the door of the boardroom open. A hand reached out and pulled the empty chair out before sliding down into it. I noticed the way Regina took note of the late arrival before moving along to the next subject. Whoever it was seemed to either be in her good graces or held enough clout within the company that she wouldn't dare acknowledge their tardiness in front of the group.

The smell of expensive cologne filled the air around me, sending an alarm straight through me. I knew that smell. I had forced it into my memory along with the voice that still rang through my head when I was alone in my room at night. There was only one man that I had been around who could smell that good, but there was absolutely no way that he was the man who was now sitting beside me. Was there?

Discreetly, I tried to turn my head to the side to get a better view, but I couldn't see much without getting caught. I picked up the pen that was lying next to the notepad in front of me and pulled it up by my temple, pretending to be focusing while using it as a shield to hide my face. His attention appeared to be on Regina, so I took the opportunity to turn my head slowly in his direction, keeping the pen up at the side of my head.

His hair was dark, way darker than I remembered it being at the club, but it still had the same mussed look he had that night. Olive-toned skin complimented the tailored navy-blue suit he was wearing that hugged his muscular body perfectly. I recognized the full, pouty lips that I had sunk my teeth into before they trailed down my neck and left a hickey that I would later have to explain to Brittany. Thankfully, my sisters had been five shots in of tequila by the time I got back to the table, so they hadn't noticed. But there was no doubt about it—this was definitely the same guy from the club.

What on earth was he doing there?!

I could feel myself starting to panic as I turned my attention back to Regina and forced myself to focus. She rambled on about a company picnic and a charity event, but I had no clue what she was actually saying because at that very moment—he turned and looked at me.

I froze in place, holding my breath while I tried to force myself to be invisible. If ever there was a time for a childhood superpower wish to come true—this was it. My heart thumped against my chest, the rush of blood pulsing in my ears as everything spun around me. Maybe he would lose interest and look away. It was likely that he wouldn't remember me from that night. I mean, it had already been two weeks, and it was really dark in the club. Plus, he probably bedded a dozen women since then. I would just be a lost face among the crowd of lovers he'd recently had.

But then his leg moved under the table, brushing against my knee in the process. I jumped at the contact, my head whipping up to look at him. Panic was etched on my face as his eyes quickly locked onto mine, confirming that he knew *exactly* who I was. Suddenly, I wasn't so sure that the contact under the table was an accident.

Shit! What was I supposed to do now? Sneak out of the room and go hide my head in shame in my apartment while I looked for another job? I sure as hell couldn't start one here after I fornicated with—whoever he was.

I tried to look away, to break this stare-down we were having, but I couldn't. He pinned me in place with that same cocky smile he had given me that night at the club, and suddenly, that same energy started coursing through me as it did that night. Amusement flashed across his face as he watched me squirm in my seat, tugging my skirt down even though it couldn't go any lower without me pulling it off completely. He rubbed his lips as he cocked his head and stared at me, a million questions appearing to run through his mind as well. But before he could say anything, Regina broke his attention by calling his name.

"Ethan, did you want to come up here and give us an update?" she asked.

My heart skipped a beat as I rushed to put everything together. If this was Roberts and Associates, and his name was Ethan, that meant he was *Ethan Roberts*… as in—my new boss.

He stood up and adjusted his jacket and tie as he walked to the front of the room, joining Regina, before addressing the room.

I could feel the heat prickle my skin as I rushed to think through what my next steps should be. I could be the coward that I wanted to be and run out of the room, never looking back as I gave up the job that I had been dreaming about for years. Or I could hold my head high and pretend that I hadn't fucked my boss in the linen closet of a nightclub while trying to get over my ex.

There wasn't much time to decide as I noticed everyone getting up to leave as the meeting ended. I smiled as politely as I could at those who passed by me, saying hi before they left. It was going to be now or never.

I held my breath when I saw Regina and Ethan approach me. I stood up, my legs shaking in the heels I was wearing as I tried to steady myself. I ran a hand down the front of my black A-line skirt and tried to wipe the sweat away from my brow so they couldn't see how frazzled I felt.

"Ethan, this is Eva Sanchez. Eva, this is Ethan Roberts," Regina said with a smile as she looked between us.

We quickly shook hands before I pulled mine back and held it stiffly at my side. There was this undeniable pull between us that made me want to reach out and touch him again, but this time, I knew better. Being this close to his orgasm-inducing body made it hard to believe that he was now my boss. I found myself looking up at him, getting lost in the dark eyes that were once again locked on me the same way they had been at the club that night.

"I have another meeting that I need to jump into. Ethan, would you mind taking Eva to her office and getting her set up? I'll check in with you guys as soon as I'm done." Regina's voice startled me, pulling me out of my trance. She smiled and walked away, not giving him a chance to respond. The door shut behind her, and an awkward silence fell between us.

"So… you're Eva," he said nonchalantly, shoving his hands into his pockets as he looked at me.

"And you're Ethan," I said, trying to force my nerves to calm down. Too late for that. "Or Mr. Roberts? I'm sorry, I shouldn't assume that I can call you Ethan… I'm not normally this chaotic, and—" I started to ramble when he lifted his hand to stop me.

"Ethan is fine." He smiled and waved his hand dismissively before walking past me to hold the door open. "Let's go get you situated in your office."

I walked beside him down the long corridor that led to the end of the hallway. Two offices sat across from each other and were separated from the other offices with a receptionist desk against one wall and an elevator on the other. It was relatively private, and I felt my stomach tighten when I thought about being by ourselves, separated from everyone else.

"Eva, this is Kate. She is our shared personal assistant. All visitors will check in with her, and she'll handle all of your incoming phone calls as well as other stuff. We'll go over all of that here in a little bit," Ethan explained before extending his hand out to indicate that he wanted me to move along and go to my office. I said a quick hello to the beautiful young girl with golden brown hair and followed him inside.

My eyes widened with surprise as I walked in and saw floor-to-ceiling windows that overlooked the city behind the large L-shaped desk that sat in the middle of the room. This was by far the biggest office that I had ever been in, let alone been able to call my own. Behind the desk, off in the corners of the room, were two large bookshelves. There was a couch against the other wall, next to a round bistro-sized table with two padded chairs that sat around it. I was still in awe when I felt him studying me.

"This office is incredible," I said, walking forward

and running my fingers along the dark wood of my desk. I slid around the back and sat down in the plush, oversized office chair, looking at the computer set up in front of me. "Why do I need two monitors?" I asked.

"You can choose whether you want to use only one or both; however, I find that having two monitors is helpful when working through cases. Once you get situated, you can decide what works best for you."

I nodded and leaned back, trying to take in everything. When I thought about this job as my dream job, I never imagined that it would be this glamorous or luxurious. As if reading my thoughts, Ethan sat down on the edge of the desk and smiled at me.

"It's a lot, but you'll get used to it."

"Thanks. Today has been filled with a lot of surprises, to say the least," I tried to joke, hoping to address the elephant in the room.

"Well, it's all business here, so we won't let our past interfere with that."

His tone had changed quickly, now sterner and more tense than a few minutes ago.

But I had to remind myself that I didn't actually know the real Ethan Roberts. I only knew the gorgeous man who fucked me in a linen closet and gave me a mind-blowing orgasm. It was evident that there were two very different versions of him, and I was going to get to know this one.

"Agreed." I pulled my shoulders back as I sat taller and tried to act like I wasn't the least bit affected by the man in front of me.

Three
Ethan

"Mr. Roberts?" Kate's voice came through the speaker of my office phone. I pressed the button to answer her. "Yes?"

"I have Brent Wallace on the line for you."

"Put him through." I waited until I heard the click, confirming that the call had been transferred.

"Good morning, Brent," I greeted as I clicked send on the email that I had been drafting. "What can I do for you this morning?"

"I wanted to let you know that I've decided to pull out of the deal with Fred," he said tiredly.

"Night clubs aren't your thing after all?" I chuckled, opening his file on my desk.

When he asked me to join him for a meeting at the club with their new owner, I knew he wouldn't end up going through with the deal. I had worked with him long enough to be able to predict what he would do before he ever did it.

What I hadn't been able to predict was how that night would go so completely differently than I had planned.

I glanced up and looked across the hallway at Eva—the bombshell from the club who ran off before I could get her name—who was sitting at her desk, laughing at something Regina had said.

"No, there's not enough money in the world that would make that deal worth it for me," he confirmed with a throaty laugh.

"Fair enough. I'll close the file on that one, but if you decide to reconsider, just—"

"I won't." His tone was sharp, and I had to bite my cheek to keep from laughing. Brent wasn't the easiest person to please, but that was part of what I loved about working with him. He knew what he wanted and was a fucking beast of a business partner.

"Do you still want me to work on Watson Investments?" I asked, looking at his other file on my desk.

"Yes. I want those shares in Starke, and that seems to be the best way to get them. I know Watson has had financial issues in the past, so that's my aim. Acquire Cody's company and boost my shares to fifty-one percent in Starke. From there, we can discuss what I plan to do with my controlling interest."

"Got it," I said as I wrote down a few notes on a piece of paper and tucked it into the file. "I'll work on this and get in touch with you soon."

I ended the call and started working on organizing the files on my desk when I heard my stomach growl. I had been so caught off guard this morning when I found out that our new hire was the same girl from the nightclub that I hadn't taken the time to grab breakfast after the meeting.

My attention had been scattered all morning, trying to focus on anything other than the beautiful woman in the office across the hall from me. Every time she shifted position in her chair, my eyes immediately focused on her long, toned legs, which were golden brown from plenty of time spent in the sun.

By noon, Kate had brought my lunch in and set it on the table. I tried to get out of the office for breaks when I could, but nothing beat the view I had of the city. The aroma floated through the air, pulling my attention away from the email that I was trying to respond to as my stomach growled loudly in the empty room. I pressed send and looked up to see Kate delivering Eva's lunch to her office. Her smile spread across her cheeks as she thanked Kate, and there was genuine sincerity in her eyes.

I pushed away from my desk and adjusted my tie. While I had been trying to avoid Eva so I could get work done, I found that I was desperately trying to find a way to spend time with her instead. She was like a drug, and now that I'd had a taste, I couldn't stop.

I walked across the hallway and leaned against her door frame, knocking on the door to get her attention. She looked up, surprised to see me there.

"Hi," she said nervously. "Did you need my help with something?"

"Actually, I was just about to take a quick break for lunch and wanted to see if you wanted to join me."

"Oh, thank you, but Kate just brought my lunch." She nodded over to the table where the take-out bag and a drink were sitting.

I attempted to grin, but it fell as flat as my attempt to play it cool. I never had to try with women—things just came naturally to me. If I had asked anyone else to join me for lunch, they would already be in my office, making a move—which was why I never invited anyone. But Eva was different. It was like she had already disregarded what had happened between us and went straight to the professional mode we briefly discussed earlier. While I respected it, I couldn't say I cared for it. Not when thoughts of what she sounded like as she came continued to play on repeat in my mind. Just because I couldn't fuck Eva anymore didn't mean I couldn't try to get to know her in a non-sexual kind of way.

"Umm…" I stammered nervously. I hated that she had this effect on me. "Let's try that again. Would you like to bring your lunch to my office so we can eat together?"

I waited while she contemplated the idea and hoped that she would say yes because she wanted to and not because she felt like she was required to as my employee.

"Okay. Sure." She pushed away from her desk and smoothed her skirt down before walking around to the front of the desk. She reached for her food at the same time I moved forward to grab it for her, forcing us into each other's arms once again. I felt her body stiffen next to mine, the scent of her vanilla perfume filling my senses as I fought the urge to lean in and inhale the intoxicating smell. She pulled back and looked up at me under her dark lashes.

"Sorry, I didn't know you were going that way," she apologized, rubbing her full lips together. *Fuck. Me.*

"Don't be. But let me grab that for you," I offered as I reached around her and grabbed the food from the table. My arm brushed against hers, sending a thrill of electricity through my body. I sucked in a deep breath and grabbed her drink, hoping that the coldness of the ice would help chill me out.

I pulled a chair out for her as we sat down at the table in my office. Her eyes were wide with amazement as she stared out the window, taking in the sight below us. It reminded me of a child seeing the tree light up in Times Square at Christmas for the first time. I grinned, loving how impressed she was with the view. Maybe it would be what lured her to my office more often.

I grabbed the bag of food that Kate had brought me and started to unpack everything, thankful that she had gone with Italian today instead of seafood. Not that this was a date, but I didn't want it to stink in here, either. Given that we needed to find a way to work together and be professional, I still couldn't force myself to stop trying to impress her, which was weird because I had never in my life worried about impressing a woman. She was different, and I found that to be more exciting than it should have been.

Finally, she broke her attention away from the window and started to unpack her lunch, which surprisingly was pasta as well. I laughed and wondered if Kate had anticipated that we would have lunch together and had ordered food from the same restaurant on purpose. She was overly receptive to people and had a knack for knowing how to coordinate things, making it all look like it was purely coincidental.

Eva opened the lid to her pasta and leaned forward, closing her eyes as she inhaled the savory aroma of her Penne Alla Vodka. The smell filled the room and mixed beautifully with the Pasta Al Pomodoro that was sitting in front of me. It was silent while we scarfed down our food, neither of us willing to stop to try to make friendly conversation.

I had to force myself to focus on my plate and not on the sounds she was making as she ate. The little whimpers paired with her closed eyes as she savored each bite were pure torture. When she held the breadstick to her mouth and licked her lips before parting them to take a bite, I nearly lost it.

My dick pressed against the fabric of my trousers as I tried desperately to think of anything other than her mouth wrapped around my cock the way it was with that breadstick. I quickly finished the last few bites before chugging my iced tea while I worked on getting my hard-on to disappear. I turned my attention to the window while my mind tried to shift to work-related topics while she finished her breadstick. Finally, a few minutes later, I heard her toss her disposable fork into the empty container and close it.

"Thanks for inviting me over for lunch," she said as she started to get up. "I should get back to my office so you can get back to work."

"You don't have to rush off, Eva. Believe it or not, we give employees a full hour for their lunch. Not the thirteen minutes it took for you to eat."

It felt odd to think about what most people did with a full-hour lunch break when I couldn't remember the last time I had stopped for more than ten minutes to eat. I did not stop to take breaks; there was always too much to get done. But I didn't want to scare her off right away and have her think that she had to be as obsessed with work as I was.

"I don't want to keep you from what you need to do," she countered, still hovering above her chair. The angle at which she was standing allowed her shirt to dip in the front, giving me the perfect view of her full breasts that were desperately trying to bust out of the white lace bra she was wearing. The same ones I had fondled in the closet before sucking her nipples.

"It's fine," I said with a little more aggression than I had intended. "Sit."

Shit. I wasn't trying to scare her or bully her into spending time with me. But she left me a flustered mess, and I was struggling to get non-sexual thoughts out at this point.

She tilted her head and looked at me, her eyes narrowing slightly. I leaned back in the padded chair and folded my hands over my stomach as I watched her sit down and cross her legs under the table. I had to play it cool, even if I was anything but right now.

"So, how are you feeling about your first day so far?" I asked, hoping the conversation would be what I needed to get my mind off of her.

"It's been good. I'm just trying to get a feel for everything. Figure out my role and what is expected of me." Her voice trailed off with a thought that she didn't say out loud.

I blew out a breath, knowing that she was still thinking about the night at the club as much as I had been. It was impossible to pretend that it hadn't happened, but it seemed to be weighing on her mind as much as it had been on mine.

"I'm happy to have Regina come by and go into more detail about your role and what our expectations are for you if you'd like." It was such a bullshit answer that made me sound like a total dick, but that was all I had right now.

"That's not what I'm talking about, and you know it." She folded her arms over her chest and continued to glare at me.

I swallowed hard, knowing full well I had met my match. Never in my life had I ever had a woman who held her own against me, especially at work.

I worked my jaw back and forth, uncomfortable with having to have this discussion. This was the main reason that I didn't bother with relationships. People start to have feelings, and then they expect you to talk about them. I stayed quiet for a few minutes while I tried to think of the easiest way to handle this conversation with the least amount of damage.

"Do you want me to quit?" Her tone was sharp, matching the look she was giving me.

I pulled my head back in surprise. Okay, that felt like it came out of left field.

"Why would I want that?"

One of the first things I learned in law school was that if you wanted to stall and get a feel for what the other person was thinking—answer their question with a question of your own. But I could already tell that Eva wasn't some girl who just barely passed law school, nor was she impressed with what I just did.

"Because it's weird and awkward between us. We had a quickie in the linen closet of a club, and now I work for you." She threw her hands up in the air. "I mean, it's not like we knew each other when it happened, but it feels weird to work for someone who's heard the noises I make when I come."

I bit the inside of my cheek to try to keep from laughing. She was cute when she was angry. I rubbed my lips together in an effort to keep from smiling before I responded.

"No, Eva, you don't need to quit. While we may know each other intimately, I expect that we can be professional and keep our personal feelings separate from work."

I hated myself for saying it as I watched the hurt flash across her face before it returned to a stoic expression. That wasn't how I felt about the situation at all, but I knew that it was the only way that we could work together and not let feelings get in the way. What I really wanted was to close the damn door and fuck her against the window while she admired the view of the city.

"Perfect," she said tightly. "Well, I better get back to my office. I'm sure my break is close to over." She stood up and pushed the chair under the table before collecting her trash and throwing it in the bin by the door. "Thank you again for asking me to join you for lunch. It was… enlightening."

She turned and walked away, leaving me and my blue balls alone in my office with the words I already regretted saying. That didn't quite go as I had hoped.

32

Four
Eva

"Your new boss is the sexy guy you fucked in the club?!" Brittany shrieked on the other end of the phone. I pulled my head away slightly, still balancing it between my shoulder and ear as I leaned over to paint my toenails.

"Yup. That's him," I said, putting the phone on speakerphone so I could finish painting the rest of my nails without having to try to balance it.

"Man! That's so wild! Does that mean that you're going to get to have hot office sex with him all the time now?"

"No," I said with a frown, even though she couldn't see it. "I don't think we'll be having any sex. This is a job, Brit, not an episode of whatever that show is you've been watching lately."

She had recently decided to binge-watch a handful of shows on Netflix and had been obsessed with telling me about the different love scenes she watched and how jealous she was that it wasn't her. She was a hopeless romantic who believed in knights in shining armor and happily ever after, while I was a realist who knew that the knights would soon be fucking their secretary on a desk from Ikea. The so-called "love" scenes she continuously raved about were the things that highly paid romance authors created when all of the realistic stories in life were covered by the evening news.

"Well, I just think that you should be more open-minded. You never know what could happen," she continued. She was clearly trying to convince me to see her side of the argument, including the pieces I had *accidentally* zoned out on while applying a clear coat of polish. I wiggled my toes in front of me and smiled. The bright magenta color of the polish made me feel less edgy as I replayed the events of the day over and over in my head.

"We talked briefly at lunch, and he made it very clear that we are to be professional with each other and leave all personal feelings at home. It wasn't the first time he had said it either," I assured her. "Trust me, there will be no sex happening between us ever again."

She sighed dramatically.

"But *if* you guys did have office sex, it could be really hot. You could say all sorts of law stuff to each other, like, *you're out of order.* Or you can *file a motion.* He might *badger your witness.*"

"Oh my god, Brit! You're so ridiculous," I said, laughing and shaking my head as I put the nail polish back on the nightstand. "No one talks like that, for one, and we don't have witnesses to badger in corporate law."

"Well, then he can badger something else… if you get my drift."

I did get her drift—more than I wanted. But entertaining those kinds of thoughts about Ethan wasn't going to do me any good. He had made himself clear multiple times today about where we stood and how nothing further would happen between us. Continuing to fantasize about him would only lead to more heartache on my end.

"Alright, well, on that note, I'm going to let you get back to another binge session of Law and Order. I'll talk to you later?" I asked, feeling drained from the day.

"Sounds good. Text me tomorrow and let me know how your second day goes. I'm going to start a bet with myself on when you guys will give in and have another quickie."

"BYE," I said loudly, cutting her off before she could continue. I heard laughing on the other end as I pressed the button to end the call.

I walked into the kitchen and pulled a frozen lasagna from the freezer, checking the cooking time before I tossed it back in. It was already late, and I wasn't in the mood to wait an hour for dinner. Instead, I fixed a bowl of cereal and sat down on the couch, flipping through the channels on the TV while my mind wandered back to Ethan.

Today had been a complete shock for me when I realized who he was. As much as I wanted to move past the fact that I had slept with my boss before knowing that he was my boss, I couldn't get the memory out of my head of how good it had been. My mind had obsessed over that night for the past two weeks, analyzing every tiny detail.

I had no idea what had come over me when I followed him to the bathroom, but for the first time in my life, I didn't regret it. How crazy was that to say—I didn't regret the quickie with the stranger in the linen closet of a packed nightclub. That's something that most people would think twice about before doing and would likely regret it later. But not me. I would do it again if he were willing to.

I could still feel the way his hands felt on my body. The way his fingers rubbed my clit so perfectly that it sent me into an orgasm within seconds. Maybe it was because I was already so aroused before he touched me, or maybe it was just because it was really that good. It wasn't like I had previous encounters with him to compare it to.

A large part of me felt disappointed when he made it clear that things between us would stay strictly professional, even though I knew that's what was best for everyone. I didn't want to risk losing my job over something silly like this. But I also couldn't stop wondering what would happen if we gave in and explored the chemistry I still felt around him. I had no idea if he felt it, too, but there were a few times throughout the day when I would feel his gaze on me, and it seemed to mess with him as much as it did me.

I had spent the better part of the morning trying to figure out how to talk to him about it and explain that I wasn't *that* kind of girl. Before him, I had never had sex with anyone who I hadn't been dating for at least a few months. I wanted to tell him that he found me on a night when I was completely vulnerable and desperate to escape what I was going through. To explain that having a gorgeous man like himself showing any interest in a girl like me was the sexiest thing I had ever seen. Allowing myself a night of uninhibited passion with a stranger was liberating and gave me the confidence I had been lacking for so long.

When Jeremy and I got together in law school, I never stopped to take a step back and make sure our relationship was what I really wanted. I didn't bother to question his change in behavior when he was promoted to a partner at his firm or the sudden power shift that seemed to go straight to his head. I also ignored the constant text messages that he would get in the middle of the night. There was so much that I had missed, and part of me wondered if I didn't care enough to notice. Maybe it was easier to stay in a relationship that I was comfortable with and that didn't require any work than to walk away and admit that I deserved better.

<u>Five</u>
Ethan

"Hey, Brent," I answered my phone, holding it between my ear and shoulder as I climbed out of the car. I gathered my things and gave a quick nod to my driver before he sped off, and I made my way toward the office. "I meant to call you yesterday, but the day got away from me. We hired a new attorney to help with some of my clients, and it took longer than expected to get her set up."

I walked briskly through the main lobby as I headed toward the private elevator in the back. Brent was quiet on the other line, which made me wonder if the call had been disconnected or if he was silent because he was pissed that I hadn't gotten back to him yesterday regarding the Watson Investments deal we had been discussing. I knew it was a high priority for him and that he was the last client that I needed to piss off right now. Or ever.

"I've been looking at every angle, and I agree that it's best not to present this as a hostile takeover— "

"Cody's dead," he interrupted. I stopped in my tracks and ran a hand through my hair. Surely, I had misheard him.

"What?"

"Dead. Died of a heart attack."

I closed my eyes and pinched the bridge of my nose. The elevator dinged beside me as the doors opened.

"Wow," I muttered, unsure of what to say. I knew that Brent and Cody had a rocky past from what he had told me, but I didn't know how this news was affecting him. While he acted cold and calculated when it came to business, the deal with Cody was more than that. It had been personal at one point in his life. "I'm so sorry to hear that."

"Yeah, me too," he sighed. I could hear the stress in his voice, the worry about what to do. "As you can imagine, this drastically changes my position with purchasing Watson Investments. On top of that, there's already a buzz about other potential takeovers."

"I'll start working on this and see what I can find out before we make a move. I'll get in touch as soon as I can with a plan."

My mind was racing with what the next steps should be as we hung up. I'd spent the morning in my office with the door closed, making calls and doing research. It turned out that Cody was more competent than I'd thought and had created an escape plan to prevent an unwanted takeover. The poison pill that he set up to allow existing shareholders to purchase additional shares at a lower price to devalue the company and make it less desirable to potential takeovers. There were several layers of ownership, and it was going to take some time to get through them all. I had to find the right person that I could talk some sense into and make this deal go the way we needed.

By noon, I had talked with a handful of people. My head was throbbing, but I had figured out a way to temporarily freeze any movement. My plan, while it would take more time than I had, was to use a white knight defense. I had spoken to the two shareholders who held the largest percentages of the company and explained what was going to happen if the company Cody had been working with took over, or worse—if another company was willing to attempt a hostile takeover. Just because Cody's Poison Pill defense had diluted the value of the shares didn't mean that the company was safe. There were plenty of greedy people in Manhattan who could care less how much money they spent to get a company that they wanted.

The white knight defense was our best option at this point, which meant that I needed to sit down and discuss with Brent what he needed to do. I sent Brent a quick text with the update and told him to stop by my office when he had a chance. I turned my attention to my email and started responding to the new ones that had come in late yesterday and were marked as urgent. I was so focused on what I was doing that I didn't see Eva walk into my office until she was standing right in front of me.

I was surprised to see that her hair was down, with long, soft waves framing her face. Her black hair made her eyes look even darker. Red lipstick was the only pop of color, and it pulled my eyes directly to her lips. I found myself staring a little longer than I should have when she cleared her throat to get my attention.

"I'm sorry," I apologized. I leaned back and ran a hand down the side of my jaw, giving her my full attention. "What can I do for you?"

"Regina suggested that I come over to see if there's anything I can help you with."

I opened my mouth to speak, to thank her for the offer before explaining that there was no way that I could stop what I was doing to delegate anything to her at this point. My Tuesday was acting like the worst Monday, and I simply didn't have the time or effort to give anything else my attention, including her. She held up her hand and stopped me.

"She said that you would have an excuse about how you're too busy to stop and let anyone help you and asked that I remind you that I was hired to work under you to assist with your workload."

She pulled her fire-red lips into a thin line and waited as she shifted her weight. Her arms were folded across her chest, which, of course, only drew my attention to her breasts.

"Well, Regina is right— I don't have time to stop. I'm glad she's well aware of it. I'm also fully aware that you were hired to work under me. I plan to implement that as soon as I'm able to."

The words rushed out of my lips faster than common sense could happen. I swallowed hard as I watched her reaction. The sudden lick of her lips before her eyes causally traveled down my body. There was no way that she hadn't heard the not-so-subtle meaning laced in my words. She blew out a slow breath and pulled her shoulders back before cocking her head to the side to look at me.

"I understand that you're busy and that you feel like the task of training me would be far too tedious for you right now. However, I have worked in corporate law for over ten years and can guarantee you that I am fully capable of handling anything you give me. Rest assured, if I have a question, I will ask you before I proceed."

I felt the frustration and tension start to drain from my body. She was right, and I knew it. I had been so focused on staying on track to make sure nothing fell in between the cracks that I hadn't even given her the chance to show me what she could or couldn't do. I wasn't treating her fairly, and I felt like a dick about it.

"Fine," I said and shrugged my shoulders. "I'm

working on a case for a client and need to have documentation outlining white knight defense. That's where—"

"A company that is being threatened with a hostile takeover seeks a friendlier firm to purchase a controlling interest before the hostile bidder can move in. The white knight tends to pay a premium above the acquirer's offer and may decide to restructure the company after the acquisition is complete in a goodwill manner to support the target company's management." She gave me a smug smile after finishing my sentence for me.

"Impressive," I replied as I nodded appreciatively.

"Brent Wallace will be by sometime today to discuss a possible takeover, and I would like to talk to him about the white knight approach. He's a brilliant businessman; however, he will want to take the information with him and run the numbers on his own. I would appreciate it if you could work on gathering the information that he will need before he gets here."

"I'm on it." Her smile briefly crossed her lips before it disappeared as she walked out of my office and closed the door.

The day sped by at an annoyingly fast pace. I remembered Kate coming in to bring me the lunch I had requested and mentioning something about someone not feeling well, but I hadn't been able to pull my attention away from the files that I had been working on to truly listen. My neck was stiff and achy as I rolled it around on my shoulders, hoping to alleviate some of the pain.

When I looked out the window behind me, the sun had already gone down, the glowing lights of skyscrapers illuminating the Manhattan skyline. I pushed away from my desk and stood up, allowing the blood to flow through my body after having been sedentary for so long this afternoon.

The clock on the wall showed it was after seven. I was surprised that I hadn't seen Brent after he had responded to my text and confirmed he would swing by to get the papers I was having Eva put together for him. I looked through the narrow window next to the door and saw that her office light was still on. It was only her second or third day—who could keep them straight at this point—so I couldn't imagine that she had work that was keeping her here late. Had she been waiting around for me?

I opened my office door and walked across the hallway, knocking lightly on hers, even though it was open. Kate was already gone for the day, which meant that Eva and I were likely the only ones still here.

"Late night?" I asked curiously when she looked up at me and smiled. She pushed a stack of files to the side and folded her hands in front of her on the desk.

"I was helping Kate with a project and didn't want to leave until I was finished."

"Is she already gone?" I pointed in the direction of Kate's desk with my finger. It was possible that she was still here if Eva was working on something for her, which also led to some increased irritation that she was assigning tasks to Eva without consulting me. Kate was Eva's assistant. Not the other way around.

"She left a few hours ago," she said casually before turning to the side and picking up the stack of files from her desk. "I told her that I would help her get these finished before the end of the day."

"Are those the minutes from the board meeting?" I nodded to the printed pages sitting on top of her pile that had been stapled in the top left corner.

"I believe so." She raised her head, extending her neck to get a look at the papers I was referring to.

"Okay." I breathed out heavily, my irritation mounting as I crossed the room to stand in front of her desk. "Why are you doing Kate's job?"

I raised my eyebrows along with my voice. I knew Kate was young, but she had worked with me long enough to know better than to pawn her work off on someone else.

"I'm not *doing her job*," she said defensively. "I'm helping out a coworker who had to leave work early because she was incredibly ill. It's the nice thing to do, in case you hadn't noticed."

I closed my eyes for a quick second, feeling more frustrated that I hadn't stopped to listen to Kate when she had popped into my office earlier.

"I had no idea that she wasn't feeling well. Did she say how long she would be out?" I asked through gritted teeth.

"At least the remainder of the week. I spoke with Regina before I took over doing the notes from the board meeting, just so you know. Kate didn't ask me to do her job." She stood up and grabbed the stack from the desk.

I nodded and stepped to the side as she pushed past me, her arms full. There were more than just the board meeting minutes in the pile, though I had no idea what else she had been working on.

"Want some help with those?" I asked, walking beside her as I tried to reach over and take a few things from the top to help her.

"I've got it. Thank you," she replied as she subtly pulled away.

I followed her around to each office as she placed a copy of the minutes on the desks and then proceeded to work her way down to the file room. The door was closed and locked, which meant that whether she wanted it or not, she would need my help. I leaned against the wall by the door and watched as she carefully tried to balance the stack of files in one arm, raising her leg slightly to try to help balance them. Her right arm fumbled around the hem of her shirt as she struggled to find her badge to swipe to open the door.

After a few minutes of persistently trying, she blew out a breath of frustration, pushing a stray piece of hair off her face. She watched me from the corner of her eye, her irritation starting to match what I was feeling a few minutes ago.

"Ready for some help?" I asked, pushing off the wall next to her.

Her eyes narrowed as she stepped back and moved out of the way while I pulled my badge out of my pocket and scanned it. The lock clicked, and I pushed the door open, making sure she was out of the way before letting it close. She made her way over to the table in the middle of the room and set the files down, the loud *thunk* echoing through the small room. Out of all the rooms on this floor, I hated this one the most because it was small, cramped, and had zero windows, which made me feel claustrophobic.

"Thank you," she muttered under her breath, reaching down to rub the red spot on her wrist where the weight of the files had dug into her skin. "I've got it from here."

"You're welcome," I answered with equal parts sincerity and sarcasm. "You don't need to file these. Leave them for Natasha. She'll be in on Friday."

"Who's Natasha?"

"Garrett's daughter. She comes to help out on Fridays and does the filing for us."

"Garrett, your brother?" She tilted her head to the

side, her face marred with confusion.

"The one and only."

"So… wouldn't that make her… your niece?"

"Well, yeah, technically it does," I said with a laugh.

I was so used to referring to Garrett in business settings that I often removed the fact that we were related when I talked about him or his family. She gave me an odd look before turning to walk out the door. Her hand reached for the handle at the same time mine did, the heat from our exchange spreading through my body. She looked up at me, her eyes darkening as our hands continued to touch. Her lips slightly parted, the moisture from her tongue glistening over them as she licked them.

The electricity continued to course through us, from her body into mine. I growled as I reached out and grabbed her, turning her back to the door as I pressed my body against hers. Slowly, I ran my hand up the back of her neck and gently tugged on her hair, pulling her head back as my lips found hers.

I intended to kiss her softly.

No, take that back. I had no intention of kissing her.

My plan was to forget that we had mind-blowing sex in the linen closet of a nightclub and move on. Be professional. But every time my body got within inches of hers, I felt this pull that I couldn't walk away from. My mouth crashed down onto hers, satisfied when I felt her lips part to invite me in. Her breathing was ragged as her hands pulled at my shirt, untucking it from my slacks.

We shouldn't be doing this.

I tried to remind myself of all the reasons why this was a bad idea as her fingers quickly worked the buttons on her shirt before tossing it to the side. Her hand slid down and grabbed my dick, my erection pushing against her.

Before I could think straight and put an end to it, I had her bent over the table with her pants and panties on the floor behind us. In record time, I had my dick sheathed in a condom and was plowing into her while she moaned against the stack of files that she had just brought in.

I wanted to take my time and devour every inch of her body, but as her pussy clenched tighter around my cock, I could tell that she wanted this as badly as I did. The way she lifted her ass and met me, thrust for thrust, confirmed that she needed it. I dug my fingers into her hips, pulling her back onto my cock as I fucked her deeper, watching as her tanned ass bounced in front of me.

She turned and looked at me over her shoulder, a look of lust on her face as my name rolled off her lips in a sexy moan. We locked eyes, and she held my gaze as I climaxed, my orgasm jolting through me. Knowing that she hadn't come yet, I slowly pulled out and turned her around to face me.

"Sit," I whispered, leaning in close to her ear while my tongue ran up the side of her neck. Her chest rose and fell heavily as her breathing got more ragged. I leaned forward and pulled the lace of her bra down with my teeth, freeing her nipples before running my tongue along them. My hand skimmed along her thigh before dipping in between and finding the wet warmth of her pussy. I slid a finger inside of her, using my hand to push her thighs further apart to allow me access as I lowered my head and pulled a hardened nipple into my mouth.

I sucked hard, flicking it with my tongue as my fingers fucked her. The way her body responded so quickly to my touch had my dick starting to get hard again. I leaned over and gave the other nipple a turn as my fingers worked their way up to her clit. I could feel her body stiffen as it reacted to the pressure that was starting to build. Her back arched, pushing her breasts further into my face as I growled and started sucking the other nipple again. I could tell that this was about to send her over the edge, and while I still wanted to taste her and devour her as she came on my face, I didn't want to ruin the pace we had when she was so close to orgasm.

I rubbed her clit harder, her chest heaving in my face as her nails scratched down my back. She tried to stifle her moan, her head tilting back as her orgasm started. Her pussy clenched around my fingers as she squirmed around me, riding the wave of pleasure while grinding against my hand. A few seconds later, she leaned forward and opened her eyes, a look of satisfaction spreading across her face.

"That was fucking incredible," I said as my eyes roamed her body, taking in every tiny detail, like the cute little mole she had right underneath her left breast.

"You're telling me," she teased while pulling her bra up and adjusting the straps. She glanced down and located the rest of her clothes. I stepped to the side and turned away as I worked to clean myself up and get dressed.

"I guess we better leave before someone walks in and finds us here."

I was just about to assure her that we didn't have to worry about that since everyone else had already left, then I remembered that I was still waiting for Brent to show up. This was the last thing that I needed to explain to him.

"Yeah, I'm still waiting on Brent Wallace to come by, so I'd better get back to my office before he shows up."

I opened the door and waited for her to go through before closing it behind us and making sure it was locked. She looked over her shoulder as she stopped and waited for me to walk beside her.

"Brent's already been by," she said, clearly confused

as to why I was still waiting.

I stopped walking, my head whipping to the side to stare at her.

"Excuse me? When did he come by?" My forehead creased as I scowled.

"This afternoon, after Kate left. I offered to come get you, but he insisted that he was in a hurry and was only stopping by to pick up the items you had left for him."

I felt like the blood was pulsing through my head, the sheer throb of it threatening to make it explode. I ran a hand down the scruff of my jawline and looked away.

"And?" I was trying my best not to take my frustration out on her.

"I gave him the documents that we had discussed earlier." She swallowed hard, the color draining from her face as she watched my reaction.

"Son of a bitch!" I growled as I turned and headed straight for my office, leaving her behind in the empty silence of the hallway. I slammed my door and paced back and forth as I tried to figure out how to fix the mess that she had just created.

Six
Eva

My head felt like it was going to explode, the pressure almost unbearable. I pulled the extra blanket from the back of the couch and wrapped it around me as I shivered. My body was achy and desperate to rest, but every time I tried to lie down in bed, my nose would start running, which would lead to a coughing fit. It seemed the only way that I could get comfortable enough to try to rest was to pile every pillow I had in my apartment and stack them together so I was at the perfect angle on the couch.

The heater was turned up as far as I was willing to let it go since I didn't need an absurdly ridiculous bill. I had taken my temperature a few hours ago and wasn't surprised that I had a fever, given how shitty I was feeling. I took some Tylenol and placed a cold washcloth on my forehead, hoping the fever would break soon. The last thing I wanted was to have to go to the doctor when I could barely get myself off of the couch.

I squirmed until I got comfortable, thankful that I was tired enough to go to sleep. But just as I closed my eyes to try to get some rest, my phone dinged with a new text message. I had already talked to Regina this morning to let her know that I wouldn't be in today, and she had assured me that she would let Ethan know.

It wasn't that I was avoiding Ethan after he had blown up at me yesterday. It was more that I would rather stick a rusty nail through my eyeball than talk to him right now. When I went by his office to talk about what had happened with Brent, I was met with ice-cold silence and was ordered to go home. I knew where I stood with him after that.

I had planned to talk to him and assure him that Brent and I spoke about what was in the folder and that I had a thorough conversation regarding what was being proposed. It was beyond irritating that he chose to treat me as if I was some brand-new lawyer, straight out of law school, when I'd been practicing as long as he had, according to Google.

I didn't bother picking up my phone to check it, nor did I bother with it when I heard it vibrating across the coffee table as it rang. My entire body hurt as I closed my eyes and tried to relax now that I had finally gotten comfortable. Within my reach was the TV remote, so I grabbed it and turned up the volume in an effort to drown out the sound of my phone as it continued to dance across the wooden surface. The sound of laughter from the show filled the room, allowing my body to give in and get the sleep that I so desperately needed.

My deep sleep was soon interrupted by the sound of someone incessantly banging on the door. Lacking the energy and strength I needed to deal with it, I lifted my hands and covered my ears as I tried to will away whoever was there.

"Come on, Eva, I know you're in there. I can hear the TV." Ethan's voice crept under the door and echoed in the small room.

"Go away. I'm sick," I muttered as loudly as I could so I wouldn't have to get up and answer the door. That was way too much work right now.

"Open the door, or I will go downstairs and get them

to give me a key. I'm not leaving until we talk," he warned.

In the short time I worked for Ethan, I knew he was one of the most persistent people I had ever met. Little did he know, I was probably one of the most stubborn people he would ever meet. I rolled my eyes and shifted my position so my back was facing the door. Within minutes, my body relaxed, and I fell back asleep. I knew it must have been a fevered dream, but it was so peaceful that I didn't mind—even if I was dancing around Times Square in my underwear to the soundtrack of *Chicago*.

I was sinking deeper into my dream, making my way through the city as I continued on my tour when I felt someone shaking my arm. I groaned and rolled over, surprised to see Ethan sitting beside me on the edge of the couch. His brow was pulled together in concern as he looked at me, his brown eyes glistening in the beam of sunlight that was forcing its way through the small gap between the curtains.

"I said go away," I mumbled and pulled my arm away.

"I'm not going anywhere until I know that you're okay," he replied with a hint of frustration.

"You're not the boss of me," I retorted, my eyes still closed with my face buried in the pillow.

"Actually, I am." He let out an amused chuckle as I felt the back of his hand press against my forehead before he muttered a couple of curse words and stood up. I could hear his voice off in the distance as he spoke, but I had no idea if he was talking to me or if he was really there. Everything was fuzzy as a chill spread through my body, making everything ache again.

Slowly, my dream started to fade as everything around me got darker. The room was quiet, and I could feel the weight of a blanket on top of me. I pulled my legs up under me and curled into the couch as I drifted in and out of sleep.

52

<u>Seven</u>
Ethan

"Get the paperwork drawn up and have it delivered to me this afternoon," I ordered before I hung up the phone. I glanced at myself in the mirror of the tiny bathroom in Eva's apartment, where I had been taking the majority of my business calls while she slept.

In the four hours I had been there, she had slept the majority of the time, tossing and turning as she struggled to get comfortable. When I decided to show up at her apartment, I was prepared to talk to her about what had happened the other day in the copy room. I hadn't meant to lose my temper with her, and she definitely didn't deserve the response she got from me. But then I found how sick she was, and I couldn't leave her if I wanted to. There was this overwhelming instinct to stay close to her and make sure she was okay.

Thankfully, I was able to convince the woman at the front desk to allow me access to her apartment so that I could do a welfare check. When Eva attempted to answer us through the front door, her words were jumbled and she sounded delirious. That was when I realized just how sick she was.

Having a mother who was a retired nurse was

helpful as she guided me on what to do to help bring Eva's temperature down, as well as what to look for before taking her to the emergency room. Her fever was high, but my mother assured me that it was okay and to let her body do what it needed to fight the illness. That didn't make it any easier watching her tremble beneath a pile of blankets or whimper in her sleep.

I was sitting in the chair across from her, working on the laptop that I had brought over earlier when she rolled over, and her eyes fluttered open. It took her a few minutes to focus before she realized that I was there. She slowly lifted herself to a sitting position and rubbed her throat before coughing.

"Why are you here?" she asked, her voice barely a whisper.

"To take care of you." I folded my hands in my lap and tried to keep the emotion out of my voice so she didn't hear how worried I had been over her. It was one thing to be concerned as her boss, but it was another to admit that my concern stretched far beyond that to a point that was inappropriate.

"Thank you, but you can go. I don't need anyone to take care of me."

She pulled her shoulders back defiantly as she tried to narrow her eyes at me. Suddenly, without warning, she sneezed. I watched as her body flinched in response, her hand grabbing her side as she tried to brace herself for the next one. She leaned forward and grabbed the box of tissues from the table before she leaned back against the couch.

"Eva, stop being so stubborn and let me take care of you," I practically begged as I set my computer on the floor beside me. I got up to get her a glass of water from the kitchen so she could take some of the medicine that I had delivered earlier. I popped a few tablets out of the package and carried them with me, waiting for her to finish sneezing before I sat down on the edge of the couch beside her. I extended my hand with the pills to her and waited for her to take them.

"What are these?" she asked suspiciously.

"Cold and flu, something or another. Sorry, I don't remember the name. I just told them to get whatever was best for the flu since that's what you seem to have. I can get the package if you want to look at it."

"You had someone deliver drugs to you?" She arched a brow as she reached out and took the pills and the glass of water from me.

"Well, that makes me sound like a drug dealer, so no—I didn't have someone deliver *drugs* to me. I had my assistant bring me medicine, as well as a few other things."

"A man with a plan," she teased quietly before taking the pills and swallowing the drink of water. "Thank you. I appreciate the medicine."

"You're welcome."

I stood up and glanced at the mess around her. There was a trashcan next to her on the floor, but it was full of tissues overflowing from the top of it. I went to the kitchen and opened the cabinet under the sink, thankful when I found the trash bags right away. I pulled one out and shook it open as I made my way back to where she was sitting on the couch. I held it in front of her, waiting for her to collect the used tissues and toss them in. I grabbed the trashcan from the floor and emptied it into the bag as well. There were a few empty Gatorade containers on the coffee table that I added to the bag before setting it by the door to take out later when I left.

"What do you feel like for dinner?" I asked, taking my place in the chair across from her again.

She scrunched her nose and shook her head.

"I'm not hungry."

"You still need to eat," I said gently, not wanting to push boundaries with her.

"I'll eat some crackers or something later." She tried to brush me off as she turned her attention to the TV to avoid looking at me.

I got up and sat on the coffee table, blocking her view as I forced her to look at me.

"Eva," I warned. "You will eat dinner one way or another. I'm not leaving here until you do. So you can either make this easy and tell me what you want, or I will decide for you. But one way or another, you will eat. Do I make myself clear?"

Color washed over her face and neck as she looked at me.

"I must really get under your skin if you think you can come into my apartment—uninvited, I might add—and tell me what to do. You might be my boss when we're at the office, but you sure as hell aren't the boss right now."

"I'm not trying to be your boss. I'm trying to make sure you're okay and that you don't end up in the emergency room because you're being too stubborn to let me take care of you," I growled, leaning forward and resting my elbows on my knees as I stared at her.

"I didn't ask you to take care of me." She threw her hands in the air in frustration.

"No. You're right. You didn't. But regardless, I'm here, Eva. And believe it or not—I care about you. Which means I can't walk out of here and leave you alone while you're sick when the least I can do is help take care of you. Please stop making it so damn difficult."

"I'm not the one who makes things difficult," she shot out, then immediately pressed her lips together to keep from talking as her eyes widened.

"What's that supposed to mean?" I asked, knowing that we were finally going to clear the air between us.

"Nothing." She folded her arms over her chest and looked away.

"Bullshit. Say what you've been wanting to say, Eva."

"I said it's nothing," she objected before she started coughing.

I grabbed the glass of water and waited until she was done before offering it to her. She side-eyed me as she took it, and I had to pretend I didn't feel the electrical currents running over my skin as her fingers brushed against mine.

"I'll order some soup and pasta from the Italian place on the corner," I said, not bothering to wait for her to object to it as I got up and walked into the kitchen to place my order.

Whether she wanted my company or not didn't matter at this point. She was obviously sick, and I was worried about her well-being, which meant it was my job to stay and make sure she was okay for as long as she needed.

By the time the food got there, Eva was asleep on the couch again. I knew that she needed her rest, but given how restless she was, I didn't feel bad waking her up to eat.

"Dinner is ready," I said softly as she glared at me and wiped the sleep from her eyes.

"I told you I would eat later."

"Yeah, and I told you that you would eat now."

It wasn't the most mature response, and it was a little

more aggressive than I would have liked, but seeing her so weak made it hard for me to care. I wanted to get her better as fast as possible because knowing she was so sick made my heart ache.

I set a bowl of soup on the table in front of her and then went back to grab the plate with pasta that I had prepared for her. I had no idea what she might like or what might upset her stomach, so I tried to go with light dishes. Overall, the goal was to nourish her body in any way I could.

"This tastes delicious," she said softly as she lifted the spoon to her mouth and took a sip of the broth. "Thank you."

"You're welcome. I wasn't sure what you liked, so I went with some of the basics. I was going to cook you dinner but didn't find much in your freezer other than ice cream and a couple of TV dinners."

"Yeah, I could've told you that you weren't going to find anything in there," she said with a laugh as she leaned back against the pillows without spilling the bowl of soup. "I come from a large family of Latin women, and I'm the only one who can't cook."

"Really?" I asked, my eyes narrowing as I waited to see if she was messing with me. It wasn't like I was all that great about keeping my freezer and fridge stocked with food, so I couldn't blame her for hers being empty. I knew what it was like to be so busy all the time that it was easier to grab takeout instead of trying to cook.

"Yep. While my mom was busy teaching my sisters to cook, I was always up in my room studying. I guess my mom just gave up on trying to domesticate me when I was more interested in school than cooking."

"Eh, there's a lot of people who don't like to cook," I offered, twirling pasta on my fork before taking a bite.

"Oh, it's not that I don't *like* to cook. I literally *cannot* cook. One time, I almost caught our kitchen on fire trying to make toast. I've also ruined macaroni and cheese so many times that no one allows me to even look at the box anymore."

"How did you almost catch the house on fire? Toasters are fairly simple to use." I quirked a brow, eager to hear how she could have possibly screwed that up.

"It wasn't all my fault. My family has a really old toaster that is built into the wall. You pull the side of it out, pop the bread in, then press the lever down and it makes the toast. *I*, however, thought it was a good idea to push the side back into the wall after I pressed the lever down. There was nowhere for the heat to go other than in the wall."

I reached up and smoothed a hand down the scruff on my face as I struggled to hide my grin. The look on her face was adorable, and I could picture her as a naïve little girl attempting to make toast without realizing what she was doing.

"Okay, that's pretty bad," I said as I laughed. "But we all do silly stuff when we're kids."

"That was just last week," she said, her tone serious and her face straight as she watched for my reaction.

I closed my eyes and bit the inside of my lip to keep from laughing.

"You're kidding, right?" I asked quickly before I lost control.

"Yeah," she said playfully, her voice still raspy. "It was two weeks ago."

I shook my head and laughed, loving that her playful side had returned.

60

BREAKING ALL THE RULES

Eight
Eva

Almost everything from the past forty-eight hours felt like a blur. I knew that it had been my fever that had made me feel delirious and caused me to question my sanity because I could have sworn that Ethan had stopped by my apartment and insisted on taking care of me. It had to be a fever dream because there was no way that we ended the day together, enjoying a warm bowl of soup and laughing when things between us had been so strained.

When I rolled over and woke up, I felt slightly relieved that I was alone and somehow had managed to get myself to bed safely last night. I got out of bed and slid on the plush, warm robe that I loved to ward off the chill I felt. My body still ached, which meant I hadn't gotten better overnight like I had hoped.

I made a quick note to check in with Regina to see how Kate was doing and to let her know that I would be out another day. I also needed to let Ethan know that Brent was planning to come by this morning to discuss things with him. But that could wait until I was actually functional this morning.

I walked down the short hallway into the living room, getting ready to head into the kitchen for a much-needed cup of coffee. I stopped in place, my heart skipping a beat, when I looked over and found Ethan stretched out, asleep on the couch. He was still wearing dress slacks, and his button-down shirt was now wrinkled and rolled up to his elbows. The jacket that went with it was hung on the back of the chair across from him, with his shoes neatly tucked underneath it.

I took a few minutes to admire his gorgeous face as he slept. For once, he looked peaceful. He wasn't frowning, and the vein in his forehead was nowhere to be found. I wondered if this was what he might look like on a good day when he was happy and not stressed at work. My mind quickly wandered back to the night when I first met him and how calm and collected he looked sitting in the VIP lounge. He definitely had a charisma about him that made people notice him, but he didn't seem to intimidate anyone the way he did when he was at the office.

A strand of his dark hair rested on his forehead, and my fingers itched to reach over and brush it away. To run them through his thick mane and feel how soft it was. While I took good care of my hair, I was also quite envious of his and wondered how much work it took for him to get that slightly mussed look. I sat down on the arm of the chair, continuing to stare at him, when suddenly his eyes fluttered open, and he looked at me. He smiled and sat up, rolling his head back across his shoulders.

"Good morning," he greeted, his voice low. "How did you sleep?"

"Good, I think. Maybe too good," I said with a soft laugh. "For a minute, I thought I had dreamt that my boss came by my apartment and fed me magical soup that healed me."

"It was better than burnt toast." He laughed and raised an eyebrow at me. I could feel the heat rush up the sides of my face, spreading quickly as I remembered a sliver of the conversation about my cooking abilities last night.

"I did NOT tell you about the burnt toast," I moaned, covering my face in my hands.

"Oh, you sure did. Amongst other things." He smiled a crooked smile, one that I hadn't seen before. It was sexy and sent a rush of warmth through my body as I imagined him grinning at me like that as he hovered over me and brought me to climax.

I waited a few minutes to see if he would tell me on his own. Instead, he got up and grabbed his cell phone from the coffee table, checking his messages while wearing a smug smile. I racked my brain, trying to remember as much as I could, but everything was really fuzzy in my head. After all, I thought I had dreamed that he was at my apartment taking care of me, and yet here he was, standing in front of me while the empty take-out containers that sat on the counter by the door. He slid his phone into his pocket and turned his attention to me.

"What else did I tell you?" I asked nervously, chewing on my fingernail. "If it was anything personal or inappropriate—I apologize now." I held my hands up in front of me.

Once the word *inappropriate* was out of my mouth, I felt the energy shift between us. We both had been avoiding talking about what had happened in the file room as much as we had avoided talking about the night we hooked up at the club. The playful side of him was gone, and I was immediately greeted by the rigid Ethan that everyone at work feared—everyone except me.

"Look, about Tuesday," he said, raking a hand through his hair as he started to pace in front of the couch. "That shouldn't have happened, and I'm sorry that it did. We work together, and our relationship needs to stay professional." His eyes went wide with embarrassment when he said *relationship*. "Not that there could be a relationship— I'm not that kind of man," he hurriedly assured me.

"Got it," I said with a hint of annoyance in my voice. "But just so we're clear— *you* came on to *me* in the file room. Not the other way around. And while it was enjoyable, I was not hired to be some booty call. I expect that we can put this behind us and that you will step aside from your ego and train me on how to do the job *you* hired me to do."

"Technically, Regina hired you," he said with a smirk that perfectly highlighted his dimples. I rolled my eyes and looked away, though I was happy to see the playful side wasn't too far from the surface after all.

"I thought you called in and were avoiding me because of what happened," he admitted, rocking back on his heels as he looked at me.

"Unfortunately, no. As much as I would have hated the guaranteed awkward tension between us, I wasn't going to put my job at stake by calling in just to avoid you. I would have been there if I could have seen straight and didn't feel like death. Which you got to see firsthand when you showed up and refused to leave." I gave him a pointed look accompanied by a playful eyebrow quirk.

He nodded in agreement.

"I'm sorry for assuming. Part of me showing up here was to talk about what happened and clear the air between us. Between the file room and the issue with Brent, I didn't want to keep having any awkwardness between us."

"And by *what happened with Brent*, you mean the whole *you losing your temper because I did my job* issue?" I questioned, narrowing my eyes at him.

"While I appreciate that you did your job, Eva, you still spoke to a client without my permission."

"Well, I'm sorry. I wasn't aware that there were limitations and stipulations on how I got the job done. Please let me know in advance what your *babysitting* role entails so I don't screw up in the future. It was my error to assume that I was free to discuss the items I worked on with the client I worked on them for. Perhaps *you* could find the time to train me so we can avoid these issues in the future."

"With all due respect, Eva, I don't have the time to spend training you, especially on something as menial as that. It should be a given that you don't speak to one of my clients without my approval. Regardless of your experience, you're still a new employee of our firm, and I have the right to monitor what you do and make sure you're doing it correctly. Respect is something that automatically comes with the territory, and you should know that given your experience."

"Okay, let's just get one thing clear— you do *not* intimidate me. I will not bow down to you or kiss your ass to make you feel better about yourself. I am a *damn good* attorney and have earned every single promotion that I have been given. I have worked my way to where I am because I am driven, motivated, and refuse to take no for an answer. I will not have you insult me by insinuating that I don't know what I'm doing when you haven't taken the time to see what I'm fully capable of. I've already apologized for my error. I will not allow you to continue to reprimand me for it."

"I'm sorry. That wasn't my intention."

"Thank you."

I swallowed hard, trying to force the nerves down as I struggled to appear unaffected by him.

"How about we agree to start over? A fresh start where we put everything behind us and move forward?" he offered, his face softening as a smile played at his lips.

"Why do I feel like there's some sort of conditions to

this that I'm not going to like?"

"There's not. We had a conflict, and now we've discussed it like adults. I don't see the point in continuing to dwell on something that no longer matters. I enjoy having you as an employee, Eva, and I feel you can bring a lot to the table."

"Wow. A compliment?"

"Don't look so surprised," he muttered. "I do have a soft side on occasion."

"Yeah, like when you stay the night at your employee's apartment to care for her when she's sick?" I offered with a genuine smile. I hated that he had spent the night here when I knew that he had things he needed to do. I hated even more that he had seen me at my absolute worst.

"For starters," he replied with a chuckle. He glanced down at his watch and blew out a heavy sigh. "I need to get to the office this morning to handle a few things. Will you be okay on your own, or do I need to confiscate your toaster before I go?"

"I'll be fine. Toast doesn't even sound good." I rolled my eyes and tried to ignore the heat washing over my cheeks.

"Alright. I'm heading out, but call if you need me."

"Thank you for everything last night. I really do appreciate it."

"No problem."

He smiled, and for a brief moment, I saw something in his eyes. A softness that I hadn't seen before. I was desperate to hang onto it a little bit longer but knew that he needed to go.

"Oh, by the way, Brent will be coming in this

morning to talk with you about the information I gave him. He didn't give me a time. However, I assumed that he's not the kind of client that I should pressure into making an appointment."

"No, definitely not. I'll be sure to have his files ready when I get to the office. Thanks for letting me know."

He gave me a quick smile before grabbing his coat off the chair and sliding his shoes on. I wondered if anyone at the office would question where he had been or why he was wearing the same suit as yesterday, especially with the wrinkles.

"Sorry! There's actually another thing," I said quickly, stopping him as his hand turned the knob to open the door. "Brent mentioned that he also needed to speak with you about Karly. I'm not sure if this is related to the same deal or not, but I thought you might want to know."

Ethan squinted his eyes as he pinched the bridge of his nose between his fingers and sighed.

"She's his ex-fiancé and left him for his best friend. The one who owned Watson Investments."

"Well, that just got messy really quickly, didn't it?"

"It sure looks like it. I'll get in touch with you this afternoon. Try to rest and recuperate. I'll need you to jump in and help with this case as soon as you can."

I closed the door and found myself smiling as I realized that he was finally coming around to me helping him.

Nine
Ethan

I rushed to the office and changed into a fresh suit before grabbing the files that I needed before Brent arrived. It felt odd not having Kate up front to keep an eye out for him. Instead, I was forced to rely on the elderly woman who had her nose pressed against the computer because she couldn't see, even with her bifocals. Between her hard hearing, inability to see anything, and her calling me *Mr. Robbins*, I was already irritated and made a note to talk to Kate about using a different temp agency in the future.

My stomach growled as I slid behind my desk, a harsh reminder that I hadn't had time to stop for coffee or breakfast on my way in. I reached over to press the button to call up to Kate's desk and then quickly removed my finger when I remembered that she wasn't there. On a whim, I went into Eva's office and checked her top drawer where I had seen her stash a few granola bars. I wasn't the kind of person who ever went through my employee's things, let alone steal food from them, but desperate times called for desperate measures.

I opened the drawer and peeked inside, relief washing over me when I saw a handful of them. I grabbed one and pulled it out, feeling a tad bit victorious, when I looked up and found Brent watching me from the hallway between our offices. He arched an eyebrow in response but said nothing. Embarrassed, I held it up in front of me and offered an awkward smile.

"Breakfast," I explained as I walked around from her desk and met him in the hallway. We shook hands quickly before heading into my office and closing the door.

"I didn't peg you as the guy who went searching for granola bars in other people's offices," Brent joked as he slid his jacket off and laid it on the back of the chair. He took the seat across from me as I walked around and sat behind the dark mahogany desk.

"Usually, I'm not." I chuckled as I moved the mouse around, the computer screen coming to life as I clicked open the files I needed. "Kate is out sick, and I didn't have time to stop for breakfast this morning."

"So, you resorted to stealing?"

I could hear him trying to keep the laughter out of his voice as he said it.

"So it would seem." I laughed and pushed the mouse to the side after I had everything pulled up. I slid the granola bar off to the side as well, hoping that my stomach wouldn't be obnoxious and embarrass me during the meeting.

Before I could speak, the door opened, and the woman from up front—whatever her name was, popped her head in and smiled. She reminded me of the warm, loving grandma who walked around with a pocket full of candy that she passed out to everyone she talked to, which made it a tad bit hard to be so annoyed with her.

"Would you boys like some coffee?" Her voice was soft and instantly made me bite my tongue. There was no need to be a dick and correct her that we weren't *boys*. We were two of Manhattan's most prestigious businessmen who people admired and respected. I waited for Brent to answer before declining her offer and waited for her to close the door as she went back to her desk.

"Alright, where were we?" I muttered, shuffling the papers beside me as I looked for the copies of the information that Eva had prepared for him.

"You were stealing other people's food while trying to get your head on straight this morning," Brent offered, leaning back against the chair as he straightened his navy blue and white pinstripe tie. "What's going on with you? You seem *different...*"

A blush quickly swept across my face, making it hard for me to deny that something, in fact, was going on. But Brent was the last person that I would confide in, even if he were offering. Our relationship was strictly business, and I wasn't about to cross that line with the only person in the world who was as much against commitment as I was.

"I'm fine. Just a little off this morning. It's always hard when Kate is out." I kept my eyes down and pretended to focus on the papers in front of me.

"You sure it has nothing to do with the beautiful new lawyer that started working for you? The one whose granola bar you're eating?"

My hand froze as my body tensed. I heard the low chuckle that escaped his throat before he shook his head. He had chosen his words perfectly and added the right tone to get the reaction out of me that he wanted.

I felt the heat spread through me, along with the panic that I had been fighting for days every time I thought about Eva. The dread that quickly followed when I had to remind myself that a relationship with her wasn't possible. No matter how great the sex was between us or how much I liked spending time with her—it didn't matter. I had to keep things professional and remember why I didn't ever allow myself to cross that line.

"Things with Eva and I are strictly professional," I lied, still refusing to meet his eyes that were fixed on me. After a few minutes, when he still hadn't said anything, I pushed the papers away and leaned back to look at him. He was smirking, and I knew that he knew.

"Alright. Fine. So maybe not *completely* professional, but we're trying not to cross that line again."

"Again?"

"We might have been together a few times." I sighed and ran a hand down my face.

Over the years, Brent had consistently confided in me, and yet, somehow, it felt oddly satisfying to do the same. Granted, his confessions were about his business endeavors, not sexual conquests. But I didn't have anyone that I was close enough with to feel comfortable discussing my personal life, and that was a lonely place to be.

"You better be careful with that," Brent warned, his tone more serious than before. "Crossing that line can have consequences you don't want."

"That's what I keep telling myself," I groaned. I hadn't been able to stop thinking about yesterday when I worked remotely from her apartment so I could take care of her, and then I spent the night making sure she was okay.

"So, what's the problem? Besides the fact that she's your employee?"

"The problem is that she's one of the most incredible women I've ever met. She's insanely brilliant, confident, assertive, and beautiful inside and out. She's the most fearless woman that I've ever met, and the few times I've made the mistake of pushing back on her, she's been quick to put me in my place. She knows what she wants and goes after it, no questions asked." A smile tugged at my lips as I remembered how Regina made Eva an offer and was met with a counteroffer for higher pay, accompanied by a detailed list of why she felt she deserved it.

"I'm not going to lie. I was rather impressed with her when we spoke on Tuesday. You have an amazing attorney working for you. Don't fuck it up." He gave me a pointed look, and I laughed.

"Gee, thanks for the vote of confidence," I joked before switching gears and getting back to business. I knew that Brent was as busy as I was, and his time wasn't something that I wasn't willing to waste.

"Speaking of your conversation, did you have any questions regarding the items she prepared for you?" I asked as I reached over and grabbed my copy. When I looked up, I found Brent giving me an odd look.

"No. Eva was very thorough when she went over the options and explained that the white knight would produce the most favorable outcome at this point. Given that other investors are looking at a hostile takeover, it would make sense to approach them with a gentler option. However, after I attended the wake, there are some new developments that we need to take into consideration before I make a decision."

A sudden sense of clarity struck me as I remembered her telling me this morning that Brent wanted to discuss something that happened with Karly.

"Eva mentioned that you wanted to speak to me about Karly," I said, taking note of the change in his posture as I mentioned her name. "I'm guessing she wants to merge Watson Investments with Wallace Financial Holdings?"

He stayed silent, and a subtle nod was the only confirmation that I was on the right path.

"From a business standpoint, it would make sense to merge them. But from a personal…"

"It would be a fucking disaster," he finished for me.

It was my turn to nod.

From the research I did on Tuesday, I knew that Karly was going to be the decision-maker for Watson since she held the majority of the shares. There was no way to avoid having to deal with Karly. I knew that when I reached out to the two board members with the next highest number of shares and planted the idea of the white knight defense in their heads. I needed them to start discussing it amongst the team and to form a solid wall that Karly couldn't get around.

"What exactly does Karly want from the deal?"

"She wants us to merge the companies and run them together. As a team," he gritted out. "I've already explained to her that it's not an option that I'm interested in, but you know Karly, she won't stop until she gets her way. She scheduled a meeting for us to discuss Watson tomorrow."

I leaned back against my chair and waited. Something else was weighing on Brent's mind, and I knew it was more than just Karly wanting to merge the companies. He was a brilliant, powerful man who made strategic, logical business decisions, but something was holding him back.

"So, what's the real problem?" I asked, pushing him to break free from his trance and look at me.

"There's a child involved."

"A child?" I pulled my head back in confusion, my brows furrowed. There hadn't been any discussion of a child before now. "Whose child?"

"Mine." His eyes locked onto mine, and I felt the weight of his problems shift to my shoulders. Fuck.

Ten
Eva

Somehow, I made it through the weekend without dying, which sounded overly dramatic, but I had never been that sick before in my life. I had no idea how Kate was feeling and if she had recovered, nor did I know if anyone else had come down with it. I prayed that it was limited to our section of the floor and that since we were so secluded, no one else had caught whatever this was.

Sunday mornings were always my favorite because I would meet up with my two sisters for brunch after a quick morning run. I felt disappointed that I had to miss it this morning—brunch—not the run. My body still felt like a semi-truck had hit it, and I had no intention of moving from the couch now that I had finally gotten comfortable.

The apartment was filled with the smell of burnt toast as I curled up under a blanket and watched a rerun on TV. I had no idea what the show was, but it was in black and white. My hand was too heavy to try to work the remote to change the channel, so I let it be and laughed at the shenanigans that the crazy woman on the screen kept getting into.

I nibbled on the edge of the piece of toast that was the least burnt and hoped I would be able to keep it down.

Ethan had taken the liberty of ordering me groceries when I called in again, knowing I wasn't going to be able to go out and get anything until I got better.

I was frustrated that I had already missed three days of work in my first week there, but it wasn't like there was anything I could do about it. Even if my stubborn ass tried to go into the office, I wouldn't have been any help given how delirious I had been with the fever the past couple of days. Thankfully, today, I was officially fever-free and hopefully on the mend.

My cell phone vibrated across the table, giving me an excuse to set down the burnt toast to grab it.

"Hey, Gabi," I said, pushing myself up on the couch. "Sorry I missed brunch. I've been super si—"

"Don't worry about brunch," she said dismissively. "We have bigger problems."

"What's wrong? Is Mom okay? Did something happen to Dad? Did he have another heart attack?" I threw the blanket off of me, ready to rush out of the house to get to my family, when a wave of dizziness washed over me.

"It's Lucy."

"What happened?"

Lucy was my baby sister, and I was more than a little overprotective of her. Not just because she was the baby of the family but because she had a prick for a husband, and she refused to accept that she deserved better. She had come to talk to me a few weeks ago, seeking legal advice after she caught him cheating on her.

"She and Lance had another fight." She sighed heavily, and I knew she was going to give me all of the unnecessary details. Unfortunately, she was the middle child who thrived on drama and gossip. "Apparently, he's been sleeping with his secretary at work, and from what I've heard, she's a real—"

"Headline news it for me, Gab," I interrupted. I didn't care about who he was sleeping with. My only concern was that my little sister and nephew were okay. "Was the fight physical?"

Lucy had been married for five years, but I had been suspicious of Lance since the day I met him. Shortly after she found out she was pregnant, Lance started changing for the worse. He was constantly on edge and hard to be around while I watched the confidence slip right out of my sister the longer they stayed together. She was convinced that she could make things work so her son didn't have to grow up without a father. I was convinced that Lance belonged six feet under.

"I'm not supposed to say," Gabi muttered into the phone, stalling.

"You're not doing her any favors by not telling me. I can't help her if I don't know what's going on."

"She came by Mom's house this morning with Jackson. She asked if they could watch him for a few hours. Her lip was busted, and she had a black eye. She tried to hide it with makeup, but I could see it. Everyone could see it."

I closed my eyes and forced out a slow, steady breath, praying that it would help calm me down. I barely had the energy to get off the couch, but this made my blood boil and gave me an adrenaline boost that I needed to take care of my family.

"Where did she go?" I asked as calmly as I could.

"She's heading to my house. Mom called me and told me right after she left."

"Okay. Once she gets there, I want you guys to come to my apartment so we can figure this out," I said as I forced myself to stand up. I immediately felt dizzy and reached down to hold onto the couch.

"Are you sure you're up for this? You sound pretty sick. I don't want to intrude."

"Gabi, stop acting like the middle child and get your ass over here. I'll see you guys in a little bit."

"Okay. We'll head over as soon as she gets here."

"And one more thing," I said quickly before she could hang up. "Grab a box of bagels and some cream cheese. I'll give you cash when you get here."

"Did you burn your toast again?" She laughed hysterically on the other end as I rolled my eyes.

"Just bring the bagels," I replied sarcastically before hanging up.

Half an hour later, I heard a knock on my door. I got up and slowly made my way to answer it, hoping I didn't lose my balance again. While I was fever-free, I was also severely dehydrated and needed food to get my strength back.

My eyes immediately went to Lucy as she kept her head lowered and fidgeted with the long sleeves of her shirt. Her lip was swollen in the corner where a scab of dried blood had formed. A bruise ran along her cheek and under her eye, making my blood pressure rise as I thought about how hard he had to hit her to leave a mark like that on her.

My heart broke as I held my arms out for her. She stepped forward into my embrace, her body trembling as she cried against my shoulder. Gabi gave me a sad, sympathetic smile as she squeezed past us and set the box of bagels on the counter. I held Lucy for a few more minutes before I gently led her inside and closed the door.

"I'm sorry to intrude when you're not feeling well," Lucy apologized quietly, tucking a strand of black hair behind her ear. I caught a glimpse of a bruise along the side of her throat that had been covered by her hair and felt my blood start to boil.

"You don't *ever* apologize for being here," I said sternly, looking her in the eyes.

"I am always your safe place." I softened my tone and gently reached over to wipe the tear that was running down her face. "I got you, Lucy. You never have to worry about coming here, okay?"

She nodded and wiped the rest of the tears with the back of her hand. We headed for the couch, and I winced as I sat, my body still sore and achy from being so sick. I noticed the concern etched on their faces as they watched me.

"I'm fine," I assured them as I fought to get comfortable. "I just need to sit down and rest for a few minutes."

"Have you eaten today?" Lucy asked as she sat down in the chair across from me.

"She burned the toast," Gabi volunteered for me as she grabbed the bagels and set them on the coffee table.

"That's what I smelled when I walked in!" Lucy laughed, offering me the same sympathetic look that I had seen her give her four-year-old plenty of times.

"Very funny," I replied, rolling my eyes as I accepted the bagel that Gabi handed to me, smothered with strawberry cream cheese.

"How are you feeling?" Lucy asked as she leaned forward to take the bagel that Gabi offered her.

"Thankfully, I'm feeling better than I was when this first started. The first few days were pretty rough." I shivered as a flashback of how terrible I had felt crossed my mind.

"Why didn't you call one of us? We would have come over to take care of you." Gabi leaned back against the couch and took a bite out of her bagel.

"Honestly, I was so sick that I couldn't even see straight. I was so delirious that I thought I had dreamt that my boss was here taking care of me," I said as I snorted, taking a bite.

"Could you imagine? That would be totally insane!" Gabi laughed as if it was the most absurd thing she had ever heard.

I swallowed hard, trying to force my bite down and keep the blush off my face. So far, Brittany was the only person I had told that Ethan was the same guy I had hooked up with at the club. I was planning to tell my sisters at brunch this morning, but then everything else happened.

Lucy narrowed her eyes and studied me.

"You're not telling us something," she accused, pointing a finger in my direction and shaking it.

"There's nothing to tell," I rushed the words out, hoping to change the subject back to her. "What we need to talk about is what happened with you and Lance."

I was *this* close to shifting the attention away from me when Gabi decided to pipe up.

"Lucy is right. Something is going on. Not only do you look guilty, but you're blushing." She stared intently at me, waiting.

"Nothing is going on," I insisted, feeling the heat spread even further across my chest and up my neck. "All you're doing is trying to make something up so we don't have to talk about the real reason why you guys are here. I know that none of us want to talk about that asshole, but we need to. We need to come up with a plan to get Lucy and Jackson out of the house and somewhere safe until the divorce and custody agreements are in place."

"Maybe we should call Brit?" Lucy offered, totally ignoring me as she looked at Gabi. "I bet she knows what's going on."

"You're right," Gabi agreed. "Brit always knows everything, sometimes before it even happens. It's like her special psychic ability or something."

Gabi pulled her phone out of her pocket, swiped her fingers across the screen a few times, and then held it in the air, facing me. Her fingers were right over the *send* button as she raised her eyebrows and challenged me.

"Fine. I was planning to tell you at brunch anyway," I muttered and rolled my eyes.

Gabi set her phone on the couch in between us as I pulled in a deep breath and instantly regretted it as I burst into a coughing fit. I took a drink of water and waited to make sure it was done before I started talking.

"Do you guys remember the guy from the nightclub?" I asked. It hadn't taken long that night for them to figure out I had hooked up with someone when I returned to the table with a slit in my skirt that hadn't been there before. While they knew I had hooked up with someone, they didn't know who he actually was.

"Mr. Tall, Dark, and a double shot of tequila?" Gabi teased and wiggled her eyebrows. "Yeah, I remember him."

Lucy laughed and nodded her head for me to continue.

"Well, it turns out that the guy from the club…" I paused and took another deep breath, more carefully this time. "Is also my new boss. Ethan Roberts."

"NO. FUCKING. WAY." Gabi clasped a hand over her mouth and stared at me in disbelief.

"Language!" Lucy scolded.

"What?!" Gabi exclaimed. "Jackson isn't even here."

Lucy's face fell as she looked around and realized that Gabi was right.

"Oops. My bad." She giggled and took another bite of her bagel.

I laughed and shook my head, enjoying the playful banter between them. Even though they were thirty-two and thirty-five, they still fought with each other like they did when they were teenagers.

"So how weird is it to work with him after you guys fucked?" Gabi asked, glancing over to Lucy, who rolled her eyes in response to the foul language.

"When I first saw him, I prayed that he wouldn't recognize me, but of course, he did. We briefly talked about it, but at the end of the day, we're both professionals, so we need to act like it. It's not like we're sitting there acting on the attraction we feel for each other. Or at least we're trying our best *not* to. Sometimes it's a little hard to avoid it." I felt the heat spread over my face again as my sisters' eyes widened.

"You had sex at work?!" they both shrieked at the same time.

I nodded, rubbing my lips together to keep from shrieking with them.

"On Tuesday, right before I left for the day."

"And you haven't seen him since?" Lucy asked.

"Obviously," Gabi said as she snorted. "She's been out sick, remember?"

"Yeah… about that," I said slowly, their eyes glued to me. "Turns out that I wasn't all that delirious and that he really did come over on Wednesday and spent the day here, taking care of me."

"He what?" Gabi asked in disbelief.

"And then he stayed the night."

Their eyes got even wider.

"But he slept on the couch," I added quickly, making sure they didn't get any ideas of us having sex while I was drunk with a fever. That was just gross.

"That's crazy," Gabi said, filling the silence that had fallen around us.

"You better be careful," she warned, and I knew that she was talking about what happened with my ex.

"This isn't anything like what happened with Jeremy," I rushed to assure her. She stayed silent and watched me. "I swear, the only similarity is that they both happen to be lawyers." I threw my hands up.

"You fell in love with Jeremy and didn't see that you deserved so much better. You let him use you to get what he wanted," Gabi said softly.

"I know," I snapped, suddenly feeling irritated with the conversation. "There's nothing to worry about because Ethan and I aren't dating. Not only that, but I've grown a lot since Jeremy and I broke up. I've learned how to be on my own, and I'm doing just fine by myself."

An awkward silence spread between us.

"Why don't we talk about Lucy?" I suggested, hoping that we could end this conversation before it got everyone pissed off at each other.

I sat in silence as Lucy and Gabi talked, filling me in on the details of what happened and what Lucy wanted to do. I made notes of the things I needed to look into for her and promised to help her find the best family law lawyer in Manhattan.

Eleven
Ethan

Having Kate and Eva out at the same time had been more stressful than I had imagined, so I was beyond ecstatic when they were both back in the office, and things felt like they were returning to normal. I was exhausted from spending the weekend at the office, working on stuff for Brent, and trying to get caught up in general. The last I'd heard from him, they were waiting for the results of a paternity test before moving forward with Watson Investments. If it turned out that the child was his, then that would impact the business deal with Karly.

I responded to the last few emails that had come in before pushing away from my desk and making my way to the board room for a meeting with Regina and Garrett. I walked into the room and felt the tension that was radiating off of them, adjusting my tie that suddenly felt too tight around my neck. They didn't bother with smiling or standing to greet me. This wasn't a meeting to discuss something good that had happened or to talk about the charity ball that we were supposed to be participating in. This was a meeting to discuss the problem that had been a thorn in my side for weeks. I took my seat and folded my hands on the table in front of me.

"Ethan," Regina said, clearing her throat. "Thank you

for meeting with us this morning. I know your schedule is very tight today."

I nodded curtly and glanced over at Garrett. He was fidgeting with his pen, a nervous habit that I very clearly remembered from our childhood after my parents split up after my father was caught cheating.

"What's the update?" I asked, cutting straight to the chase.

"Cora is filing a sexual harassment lawsuit," Regina said with a heavy sigh, pushing a stack of papers across the table to me. I reached over and took them.

"I'll let you look over the paperwork when you have the time—and I need you to *make* the time. But long story short, she's claiming that you forced her to have sex with you in the board room after hours in exchange for the raise she was given." Regina leaned back in her chair and tapped her pen on the table.

I discreetly glanced around, looking at the floor-to-ceiling glass windows that surrounded the room, and recalled the night that Cora and I had stayed late to work on a case. The day had been long and exhausting, the frustration of the week overwhelming. Cora hadn't worked for Roberts and Associates that long before she was assigned to help me with the case I was working on. She was eager to help, to say the least, but I didn't have time to stop and question what her motives were before she was under the table, sucking my dick in an effort to help me relax.

Did I know better?

Fuck yeah, I did.

Was I thinking clearly?

Obviously not.

A sloppy blow job had quickly turned into her hiking

up her skirt and bending over the table. She watched me over her shoulder as she slid her fingers through her slit, showing me how wet her pussy was. It didn't take long before my dick was inside of her, and I was questioning how we got there in the first place.

I'd been with plenty of women in my life and had never met someone as determined to have sex with me as Cora. That was the first red flag that I should have seen had I been paying attention.

The next day, things went from good—or I guess I should say *mediocre*—to bad. She came into my office and closed the door before she started to unbutton her shirt. When I told her no, something inside of her snapped, and she became this evil woman that I couldn't get rid of. I'd tried to keep things professional and keep my distance from her, but she was persistent. When I realized that she had started to become obsessed, I asked Regina to give her a raise and *promote* her to a position on Garrett's team.

I looked at the stack of papers, the regret of that night sinking in my stomach.

"I can read through all of this, but we already know that it's my word against hers. And honestly, given that we did have sex after hours, I don't know any judge who isn't going to rule in her favor. So, what options do we have at this point?" I asked, pushing the papers away from me.

"I'm working with our legal team to find out. As soon as I know, I'll let you know," she assured me. "Until then, I suggest keeping your head down and proceed with business as usual. Keep your office door open for any meetings you have, and if you need privacy for a client, have Eva or another attorney present for it."

I glanced over at Garrett and found him watching me, a lack of expression on his face. I wondered if he was sitting there, judging me, thinking that his little brother had turned into a sex-crazed pervert, just like our dad. Garrett and I had never been close, probably because he was ten years older than me, but I always felt like he resented me for something I wasn't even aware of.

I blew out a breath and thought about how all of this could blow up in my face even further if anyone found out about me and Eva. What had happened with Cora was a mistake, and I regretted it as soon as it happened. I wasn't the kind of guy who ever mixed business and pleasure. With so much at stake in the lawsuit with Cora, I couldn't risk anyone finding out what had happened between Eva and me.

The problem was that with Eva, it was different. No matter how hard I tried, I couldn't stay away from her, and that scared the shit out of me.

Twelve
Eva

Ethan had been tied up the majority of the morning in a meeting with Regina and Garrett, so I hadn't had a chance to check in with him to see what he needed me to help with. I sat at my desk and checked my emails. There were a few office updates from Regina, an offer for a beauty product that would make me look ten years younger, and a pill that could increase the size of my penis. I deleted the spam emails and allowed my mouse to hover over the email that promised to make me look younger. It couldn't hurt…

By noon, I had expected Ethan to make it back to his office, but he hadn't. I debated on whether I should take my lunch so I wasn't just sitting around on the clock, twiddling my fingers. But what if he needed something from me when he got back, and I wasn't there? I opened a new browser on my computer and began looking at food delivery options when I saw a woman walk down the hallway toward his office.

I pushed away from my desk and straightened my skirt before walking out to greet her. I had no idea if he was expecting a client today, but since Kate wasn't at her desk, I didn't want to let someone in his office while he wasn't there.

"Hi, can I help you?" I asked, pulling her attention to me as she turned around.

She was downright stunning, with olive-toned skin and long, silky black hair that flowed down her back. She tilted her head to the side for a moment, studying me before she spoke.

"You're not Cora," she said matter-of-factly.

"No, ma'am. I'm Eva." I extended my hand and waited for her to shift the box in her hand to her hip before she reached over and shook it.

"Mr. Roberts is in a meeting. Is there something that I can help you with?" I asked, watching as she turned around and put the box on his desk. It was neatly covered in red wrapping paper with a black bow fixed to the top of it. She pulled back and looked at it before reaching over and straightening it so it was lined up perfectly in front of his computer.

"I want to make sure he sees it," she said as she laughed and nodded at the box.

"I'll make sure he sees it," I assured her with a smile.

It was apparent that she knew him and that she was comfortable making herself at home in his office as she sat down at his desk and straightened the stack of papers on the side of it. I didn't know what to do at that point.

"Hello, Mom," Ethan said as he gently touched the small of my back and slid in beside me. He walked over and hugged her as she extended her arms to him.

"Happy birthday," she said cheerfully, cupping his cheeks with her hands.

I smiled and lowered my head, giving them privacy as I turned and went back to my office. I sat behind my desk, scrolling through the list of food options that I had started looking at before she came in, while occasionally letting my eyes wander to his office.

I couldn't hear what they were talking about, but I felt butterflies in my stomach when I saw how much his eyes lit up as he laughed at whatever she had said. Her hand held onto his arm for a few minutes as she continued with her story, followed by more laughter that flowed out of his office and softly flittered through mine. I felt guilty for watching them, even though I was trying not to.

Unsure of what to do, I got up to check in with Kate, frowning when I realized she wasn't back yet. My stomach growled, reminding me that I needed to eat. I still had the option of ordering food for delivery, but that would require me to go back to my office, which I was now trying to avoid. I could leave and go grab something but I had left my purse and wallet in my desk, so that wasn't an option either. I walked around aimlessly for a few minutes, wandering through the halls before I heard Ethan's voice coming toward me.

When I looked up, I saw him walking with his mom down the hallway to the lobby where the elevators were located. Once they rounded the corner and were out of sight, I made a beeline back to my office. A few minutes later, I heard Ethan coming, so I forced myself to look busy while I scrolled through the different Chinese food delivery options.

My stomach was still a little queasy, and I had since developed a strong addiction to chicken noodle soup. However, I could easily be persuaded to devour a bowl of egg drop soup if that meant that I got food in me faster. There were only two restaurants close by that served chicken noodle soup, and their estimated wait time for delivery was forty-five minutes, whereas there were fifteen Chinese food vendors that could deliver to me within ten minutes.

"Hey, how are you feeling?" Ethan asked as he leaned against my door and crossed one ankle over the other. He looked devilishly handsome in his fitted suit, which showed what I assumed was a perfect body underneath.

"I'm feeling better, but not one hundred percent yet," I answered, turning to look at him. "I was actually just getting ready to order some take-out. Do you want anything?"

"That depends." He furrowed his brow. "Where are you getting food from?"

I turned back to my computer and leaned forward a little to read the name at the top of the list.

"Happy Noodles?"

"Um. No." He shook his head and chuckled softly. "I'm not eating there, and neither are you. Grab your purse. I'm taking you to lunch."

He pushed off from the door and walked into his office. I opened my bottom desk drawer and pulled out my purse, sliding it up my arm as I grabbed my cell phone from my desk. I walked into his office and waited for him.

He was bending over his desk, looking at something on his computer, completely oblivious to the box underneath him. Surely his mom had told him about it. While I got the immediate feeling that she didn't like me, it didn't make me feel any less guilty about not telling him about the box when I told her that I would make sure he saw it.

"Your mom brought you something," I said, nodding to the box.

He glanced down at it and smiled, briefly turning his attention back to the computer before pushing his mouse to the side and picking up the box. He held it in his hands, staring at it with a small smile.

"Happy birthday," I added, remembering that his mom had wished him one.

"I overheard your mom," I explained, suddenly feeling self-conscious about eavesdropping.

"Thank you." He sighed and held the box between two hands before looking at me. "It's a gift from my grandma."

"That's really sweet," I said softly.

He nodded and closed his eyes for a second.

"She passed away last year from a heart attack." He paused for a moment before he continued. "She never missed mine or my brother's birthday. Every year, she would bake us a cake and would always pick the perfect gift for us. Half the time, *I* didn't even know what I wanted, let alone needed. But she always knew."

"I'm so sorry for your loss. She sounds like she was an amazing grandmother."

"She was the best." His voice sounded strained as he looked away, avoiding eye contact.

"My mom told me that my grandma knew that she wasn't going to make it to my next birthday. She just had a gut feeling that her time would come before then. She was determined to give us one last gift," he said as he lifted the box in the air.

"I can give you some privacy if you want to open it," I offered, turning to go back to my office.

"That's okay, you don't have to." He shook his head, setting the box down on his desk where he had found it. He pulled in a deep breath and then puffed his cheeks with air as he slowly let it out. I could see his fingers tremble slightly as they worked to open the box.

I could feel the weight of the emotions that were rushing over him and desperately wanted to go over and hug him. He slowly opened the lid to the box and looked inside.

A sad smile spread across his face as he picked up the piece of paper that was lying on top and read it.

I kept my place at the door, staying quiet so I didn't ruin his moment. A few seconds later, he laughed and looked over at me.

"What is it?" I asked.

He reached inside, pulled out a jar of peanut butter, and set it on his desk. Next, he pulled out a package of marshmallows, a box of graham crackers, and a handful of chocolate bars, setting them in front of his keyboard.

"When I was six years old, my parents separated after my mom found out that my dad was having an affair. We moved in with my grandma while my mom tried to get back on her feet. I was too little to understand what was going on or why everyone was constantly so mad and yelling at each other. One day, my parents were having a massive fight when my dad came to my grandma's to talk to my mom. They just kept yelling at each other non-stop for what felt like hours. My brother was sixteen at the time, so he left with his friends, and I was stuck there by myself." He stopped for a second and clenched his jaw at the memory.

"I was hiding under the kitchen table when my grandma came home and found me. She didn't know that my dad had come by or that my parents had been fighting, but once she saw me, she knew that something had happened. I was so scared to come out that she had to lure me with chocolate. After I finally came out, she sat me down at the kitchen table and went to the pantry to get the stuff she needed to make s'mores."

I smiled as I listened, loving the connection that he shared with his grandma.

"As I got older, my parents were constantly at each other's throats, and I wasn't shielded from it. My brother was off getting into trouble of his own, and I was left to fend for myself. Every time my parents had a blowout, my grandma would sit with me in the kitchen, and we would make s'mores. One day, when the fighting was the worst I had ever seen, she grabbed a jar of peanut butter and added it to our pile. She said, 'sometimes in life, the messier things get, the better they are in the end'. And from that day on, we never ate s'mores without peanut butter."

"That's an incredible story," I said quietly. "And I totally get it. I would never have thought of adding peanut butter to something that's already messy, but I love the way she looked at it. The mess is totally worth how delicious it must be."

"Indeed, it is," he replied as he started loading everything back into the box.

"So, where does the birthday boy want to go for lunch?" I asked when he was finished, hoping to lighten his mood.

"Do you like sushi?" he asked, following behind me as we walked out of the office. I waited while he pulled the door closed behind him and locked it. I debated whether to say no, that I couldn't stand the thought of eating raw fish, but I didn't want to ruin his lunch since it was his birthday. He laughed and playfully nudged my arm with his elbow as we waited for the door to the private elevator to open.

"I'm just teasing," he said as we stepped inside. "I would never take you for sushi when you are barely holding food down. But I do know a place a couple of blocks away that has the best egg drop soup. If that doesn't sound good, there's a cozy little diner across the street from it that should have chicken noodle soup."

"Both sound good to me," I said cheerfully. "You're the birthday boy, so whatever you want to eat is fine with me."

The words felt heavy on my tongue as I realized

just how bad they sounded. While I hadn't meant anything by it, I knew he picked up on it the second I looked at him. His eyes darkened as he worked his jaw back and forth in frustration.

"We shouldn't be doing this," he growled before he turned and wrapped his hand around my waist, pushing me back against the wall.

His mouth was on mine, his tongue swiping across my lips as it begged for access. My chest heaved as my fingers scratched at his chest, eager to touch him.

And just as suddenly as the kiss started, it ended when the bell chimed, and the doors opened to the lobby downstairs.

We pulled apart and stepped out of the elevator before anyone could see us.

My lips tingled as my fingers brushed over them lightly, desperate to feel his mouth on them again. The problem was that we weren't supposed to be doing this. We both knew that nothing could happen as long as we worked together, yet it was nearly impossible for us to stay away from each other. We knew the rules, yet we couldn't stop breaking them.

Thirteen
Ethan

"How's your soup?" I asked before lifting my club sandwich to my mouth and taking a bite. The diner was busy with a line out the door. Thankfully, we snuck in right as another table had cleared out and were given the last empty booth before the rush popped in. I wasn't sure whether Eva was in the mood for Chinese food or, rather, egg drop soup, but it didn't matter either way since the restaurant was closed due to a pipe that had burst this morning.

"It's delicious," she replied, spooning another bite into her mouth. I glanced at her lips, remembering our kiss in the elevator. The kiss that shouldn't have happened, yet it did. I was feeling incredibly frustrated with myself for it and knew that I needed to do something about my attraction to her before it was too late. There was too much at risk right now, and I couldn't jeopardize my career because my dick refused to stay down when she was around.

We ate in silence. I tried to convince myself that it was because we were starving, that it had nothing to do with what had happened. It was the constant elephant in the room that we couldn't seem to get around. I was debating whether or not to take the time while we were out of the office to talk about it when I felt my phone vibrate against my thigh in my pocket.

I pulled it out and found a text message from Brent confirming they had gotten the paternity test results back a few minutes ago, and the child was his. I ran a hand down the scruff on my face and closed my eyes. I needed to reach out to him once I was back at the office and see how he was doing with all of this.

"Is everything okay?" Eva asked, pushing her empty soup bowl to the side and taking a drink of water. I set my phone down and leaned back against the booth.

"Yeah, Brent got the paternity test results back. Chloe is his biological daughter." I had caught Eva up on everything briefly when we first got to the diner, hoping to fill some of the awkward tension between us with conversation.

"Wow. How's he taking the news?"

"I'm not sure. I'll call him when we get back to the office and check in."

"How will this affect his decision on Watson Investments?" she asked, leaning back and laying her head against the padded seat of the booth. I was happy to see that she seemed to be feeling better, but she still looked exhausted.

"I can't imagine that it will have that much of an impact other than Brent dealing with the details of his estate and updating beneficiaries. He still wants Watson Investments so he can gain the twenty-three percent stake in Starke Industries which will give him fifty-one percent ownership and controlling interest. That's what he's been after all along." I bit into a french fry and watched as her eyes narrowed at me.

"I thought he was holding off on deciding until he knew whether or not she was his biological daughter?"

"He was." I wasn't sure where she was going with this or why she suddenly seemed so angry.

"Then why isn't he concerned about doing what's right for her mother? Does he just plan to take her away from her and raise her on his own? Forget the mom because his money can buy him whatever he wants?!" She slammed her fist down on the table, glancing up to look at the few heads that had turned to see what the commotion was about.

"I don't think Brent cares about doing what's right for Karly after she cheated on him with his best friend and kept the fact that they had a child together hidden for four years," I responded sternly as I watched her.

"So, she made a mistake. That doesn't mean that he shouldn't do what's in the best interest of both of them. If he really cared about his daughter, he would make sure that her mother was taken care of instead of putting his own selfish needs first."

I put my hands up in front of me to stop her before she went off again.

"Where is this coming from?" I asked, narrowing my eyes at her.

She shook her head and looked off to the side, avoiding eye contact with me. There was something personal about this. I could feel it. It didn't make sense otherwise, given that we worked in corporate law, and our main objective was to help Brent with the business deal of purchasing Watson Investments.

"Eva," I pried, forcing her attention back to me when she refused to answer. "What's going on?"

"Nothing." She worked her jaw back and forth. "I'm just really sick of wealthy men thinking that they can control women by throwing their money around to get what they want. Especially when there is a child involved."

"In all fairness, you don't even know Brent. You don't know what kind of person he is."

"He's cocky and arrogant. That's all I need to know."

I raised an eyebrow at her as she looked away again and folded her arms across her chest.

"Well, if that's the case, then I'll gladly ask Regina to reconsider your position."

I watched as she whipped her head around to glare at me, the heat of her anger radiating off her.

"You're going to fire me because I don't agree with you?"

"No, Eva. However, I do feel that if you're unable to do the job that you were hired for because you're unable to separate your personal feelings, then maybe we need to reconsider whether you're the best fit for us. We work in corporate law, Eva, not family law. What Brent decides to do with Karly and any custody arrangements is none of our business. Our job is to guide him with the purchase of the company and move on. If you're not able to do that, then you need to let me know now."

Her nostrils flared as she exhaled, continuing to glare at me.

"I'm fully capable of doing my job," she bit out.

"Good," I said as I grabbed the check from the corner of the table after the waitress dropped it off. I glanced at it, then pulled a few twenties from my wallet and threw them on the table.

"Then let's get back to work." I stood up and walked out of the diner, unsure of whether she was coming behind me.

Fourteen
Eva

I had spent the rest of the week avoiding Ethan, even though I knew that I needed to apologize to him. The deal with Brent and Karly was really getting under my skin, and I knew that it was because of everything happening with my sister. The last update that I had from Lucy confirmed that Lance was picking up Jackson this afternoon and taking him for the weekend, while Lucy picked up a few shifts at the hospital where she worked as a receptionist. She assured me that they were trying to remain civil with each other, but Gabi had told me that it had been nothing but constant fighting.

My mind tried to separate what was happening with Lucy from what was happening with Brent, but all I could see was a rich man throwing around his money until he got what he wanted. For Brent, it was purchasing the company—which technically was Karly's now, and taking it from her without worrying about how she would continue to take care of her daughter. With Lance, he had already met with one of the most aggressive family law lawyers in Manhattan who jumped at the opportunity to take his case. Money didn't mean a damn thing to Lance, and he would pay whatever he needed to if it meant that he kept Lucy right where he wanted her.

It was almost five o'clock, and I watched as Kate packed up her stuff to leave for the day. Ethan was still in his office, head down as he read through the stack of papers on his desk. I felt bad for ruining his birthday lunch the other day and hated that it had already taken me this long to apologize. My temper had always gotten the better of me, and it was worse when my family was involved.

I pushed away from my desk and pulled at the hem of my skirt, making sure it wasn't stuck to my ass before walking over to his office. I tapped on the door, waiting for him to invite me in so I didn't overstep any boundaries. He looked up, a brief look of happiness on his face that was immediately replaced with something that I couldn't read. Maybe anger? Possibly frustration? It was hard to tell.

"Do you have a minute?" I asked, looking down the hallway as the last few people cleared out of their offices and waited in the lobby for the elevator.

"Sure," he said as he dropped the piece of paper he was looking at and leaned back in his chair. He looked so confident and collected, which made me feel even more nervous and anxious.

"I wanted to apologize for the other day," I said quietly, fidgeting with my fingers as I looked down. "I was out of line, and I didn't mean to ruin lunch."

"Don't worry about it," he said coolly, then went back to the stack of papers on his desk.

I could feel my irritation growing at his lack of interest and the way he was blowing me off. I was genuinely trying to apologize, and he was acting like an ass about it. My foot tapped on the carpet as I stood in the doorway, staring at him.

"Is there something else that I can help you with?" he asked without looking up at me.

"You really have some nerve, you know that?" I blurted out angrily.

"Excuse me?" He let the paper fall from his hands as he stood up and leaned over the desk to look at me.

"I'm standing here, trying to apologize, but you barely even acknowledge me." I folded my arms over my chest and straightened my spine.

"What exactly were you wanting from this?" He raised his brows. "You apologized. I said it was fine. Yet, you're still not happy with it." He stood upright and held his hands up in front of him. "Tell me what I'm missing here."

"Nothing," I said with an edge of irritation in my voice. "Just forget about it."

I turned to walk back to my office when I heard his footsteps behind me. In one swift movement, he grabbed my arm, spun me around, and pressed my back against the door.

"What do you want, Eva?" His eyes searched mine as he held me there, our bodies inches away from each other.

"I want you to care!" I exclaimed, feeling all of the pent-up frustration from the past few weeks suddenly coming to the surface. "Stop dismissing me and everything that happens between us, and just *care* for once!"

"I do care, Eva," he growled, stepping closer to me. "I care so much that it takes everything inside of me to try to stay away from you."

I swallowed hard, the air around us hot and thick. My chest heaved as the scent of his cologne filled my senses, making me want to reach out and touch him.

"Maybe you should stop trying," I whispered.

"I'm not good for you, Eva," he countered, leaning his forehead against mine and closing his eyes. "You'd be smart to walk away from me and never look back."

"You don't scare me," I said, grabbing his face in my hands and turning it to look at me.

Our eyes locked onto each other, and I knew there was no going back.

I wrapped my arms around his neck, pulling him into me as my lips brushed against his. He groaned as his hand slid around my waist, pulling me into the office before pushing the door closed with his foot. His hands slid down, grabbing my ass as he pushed my skirt up. We worked quickly, too frenzied, as I struggled to undo the buttons on his dress shirt.

Within seconds, it was completely unbuttoned, revealing his perfectly sculpted abs and tanned skin. I stepped back for a second to admire his body as he pulled the shirt off and tossed it to the floor. He kicked off his shoes before undoing his black leather belt, his fingers moving slowly as he watched me study his every movement.

"Take off your shirt," he commanded, pulling his belt through the loops and then holding it in his hand. I chewed my bottom lip as I watched him fold it in half before whipping it across his palm to get my attention. I reached down and pulled the bottom of my black silk tank top up and over my head. His eyes traveled down my body while he licked his lips.

"What next?" I pleaded, enjoying the way he was looking at me.

"Take off your skirt, then turn and face the window."

I glanced behind me, taking in the wall of floor-to-ceiling windows that would surely give anyone in one of the neighboring buildings the perfect view of what we were about to do.

"But what if someone sees us?" I asked nervously, slowly walking over to the window. He stalked toward me, a look of hunger in his eyes that instantly turned me on.

"Then they can watch us."

I smiled at him over my shoulder, loving the thought of it happening. I reached behind and unzipped my skirt before letting it fall to the floor. I stepped out of it, spreading my legs slightly as I balanced on my stiletto heels and adjusted my black lace thong that matched my bra.

"Fucking beautiful," he purred in my ear as he came up behind me, the hard thickness of his erection poking into my ass through his pants as he pulled my body against him.

"Put your hands on the window and spread your legs," he instructed, his voice gruff as he stepped back and I instantly missed his touch.

I did as he asked, making sure to pop my ass out for him. I grinned when I heard a low growl deep in his throat, loving that he was as turned on as I was. If I thought we were breaking the rules before, we were completely throwing them out the window we were about to fuck against.

I looked over my shoulder to see what was taking him so long and found his eyes on me, watching relentlessly as he held his belt in his hands. Without breaking eye contact, he pulled it tight and whipped it across his palm. I let out a quick gasp, my body instantly reacting to it.

"Do you like that sound?" he asked quietly, his voice low in my ear as he stood behind me again. "Does the thought of me spanking you make you wet?"

"Yes," I panted, closing my eyes and arching my back against his chest. He let out a low chuckle as he pulled back and whipped the belt across my bare ass cheek. I gasped and jumped at the same time, the sting of it surprisingly arousing.

"Fuck, Eva," he moaned and stepped away from me. A few seconds later, I heard his pants drop to the floor and the sound of foil tearing as he opened a condom before he set it on the desk beside us. I let out a soft sigh of relief and started to relax when I felt the sting of the belt on the other ass cheek this time. I tilted my head back and let out a moan.

"I never would have thought you were the kind of girl who was into being spanked," he teased as he stood behind me.

The belt fell to the floor as his hands eagerly roamed over my body, sliding up my back to undo my bra. His fingers gently pulled the straps down before tossing it behind us, then quickly moved to the front as he played with my pebbled nipples.

"I didn't know I was into it either," I admitted sheepishly.

"I can't wait to see what else you like," he murmured.

I let my head roll back against his chest while his fingers trailed across my nipples, then moved lower along my stomach. My legs parted willingly, the heat rolling off of me as he dipped his hand into my panties. He hadn't even touched me yet, and I felt like I was going to explode.

"You're so fucking wet," he panted.

I didn't say anything as I spread my legs even further, allowing him full access as his fingers plunged inside of me. I could feel his erection getting harder as it pressed against my lower back. I wanted him inside of me as much as I wanted the orgasm he was teasing me with.

"That feels so good," I cried out, panting heavily as his fingers moved faster, the angle allowing them to rub my clit. "Don't stop."

"Not a chance."

He worked his fingers against my clit, drawing every tiny bit of my orgasm out of me as I shuddered against his chest and allowed him to hold me upright until I could stand on my own. He kissed the back of my neck and down my shoulder as I came down from that incredible high. But I still wanted more.

I reached behind me and rubbed his erection, needing it to be inside of me. He growled as he gently pushed me forward so my hands were braced against the window again while he took the time to roll the condom on. He grabbed my hips and held me steady before slowly pushing inside. His cock stretched me, making me feel fuller than I had ever felt before. Then he slammed into me, bringing me to see stars from how amazing he felt as he fucked me thoroughly against the window for all to see.

I had no idea whether anyone could actually see us, but I didn't care. Sex with Ethan was addictive, and I wasn't about to stop when things felt this fucking good.

<u>Fifteen</u>
Ethan

Saturday morning was busier than expected after I squeezed in running an extra mile to try to burn off some of the mounting frustration I was dealing with before I rushed to my mom's. Having sex with Eva in my office last night was unexpected, and while it was mind-blowingly amazing, I knew that I couldn't keep doing this. I was putting everything on the line and risking my career by messing around with her at work. The last thing I needed was to wind up in another situation like the one I was currently in with Cora.

I snuck in the front door of my mom's house, glancing down at my watch to confirm that I was already fifteen minutes late. Mom had put together a brunch this morning for my birthday and informed Garrett and me that we would all be here, no matter how busy we claimed to be. My mother was a force to be reckoned with, and very few people got away with telling her no. My brother and I were no exceptions, which meant we knew we were expected to be there today, whether we wanted to or not.

While I technically stopped celebrating my birthday years ago, I found it hard to push back on my mom when she so desperately wanted to celebrate it. I had kept the tradition alive for my grandma, but now that she was gone, I didn't really see why we needed to keep it going. But I also knew better than to push my mom into something, especially when she was still grieving the loss of her mother. It was a slight pain in my ass, but I would take it if it meant that my mother was happy.

"Hey, Ma," I said as I walked into the kitchen. I leaned in and hugged her from the side before kissing her cheek and stepping away so she didn't burn herself with the grease in the pan from the bacon. "Sorry I'm late. It's been a busy morning."

"Take your seat at the table. The food will be ready soon," she replied, glancing over her shoulder. "Garrett, grab the girls and have them wash up. We're eating as a family this morning, and I'm not about to serve cold food."

Garrett mumbled something under his breath before pushing away from the table to go get the girls. Not that it was hard to find them. They were thirteen and fifteen, which meant they were likely sitting on the couch in the living room, glued to their phones—something my mother hated.

"Can I help with anything?" I offered my mother, feeling bad that she was going through all this work for me.

"Don't be silly," she scolded, "I'm not having you help with your birthday brunch."

"While I appreciate the effort, I'm not a kid anymore. I can help and make things a little easier for you since you are going through all of this work for me."

"I wouldn't do it if I didn't want to. Now sit down so we can eat."

I nodded and pressed my lips together to keep from saying anything else. By the time my mother got the food plated and on the table, Garrett and the girls had taken their seats. My mother beamed as she smiled at her family, all seated around the table and ready to enjoy a meal together.

She sat down, and the sunlight pouring in from the small window above the sink caught her face. Before she could look away, I noticed faint circles under her eyes that she had tried to hide with makeup. I frowned as I worried about whether or not she was getting any sleep these days. She had been dealing with my grandmother's estate for so long that I wasn't sure she would ever be done with it. By the looks of it, it was really taking its toll on her.

"Are you feeling okay?" I asked quietly as Garrett leaned in to scold the girls for having their phones at the table. There were heavy sighs as he took them and handed them to his wife before she put them in her purse. I smiled at my nieces and didn't take it personally when all I got in return was a forced smile from Natasha. I didn't bother to poke the bear, especially since I needed to talk to Garrett about the filing Natasha was supposed to be doing for us but wasn't.

"I'm fine," she said with a smile, though the words sounded forced.

She turned and smiled at the girls as she pulled a linen napkin from beside her plate and laid it on her lap. She waited a few minutes for everyone else to do the same before she reached her hands out to her sides to lead us in prayer. I closed my eyes and listened, feeling the cold, limp feel of Natasha's hand in mine. I chuckled, earning a tight squeeze on my other hand from my mom in response.

Once the prayer was finished, the silence in the room was replaced by metal serving utensils scraping against the dishes as everyone began serving themselves. I couldn't remember the last time I had stopped and enjoyed a meal with my family. Between Garrett and me, we always had something pressing to do that kept us from committing to anything. For me, it was usually long hours spent in the office, while for him, it was a constantly busy schedule of getting the girls to whatever extracurricular activity they were currently involved in.

Brunch flew by, and the next thing I knew, I was thanking everyone for the gifts as Garrett and his family rushed off to get to one of the girls' sporting events. I helped my mom clean up, though she fought me every step of the way. I didn't want to leave her alone in the empty house by herself, but I was also terrible company, with my mind constantly wandering to thoughts of Eva.

I knew I needed to reach out and talk to her about what happened last night, but the words were jumbled in my head. How could I tell her that I absolutely loved fucking her while also reminding her that we needed to stop? I was the world's biggest hypocrite by saying one thing and then doing the complete opposite.

But with Eva, things were different. She wasn't just some girl that I was fucking. She was someone who I was genuinely interested in, even if she was off limits. I knew we were breaking all the rules every time we crossed that line—especially at work, yet I couldn't seem to stop.

And it wasn't like it was *just me* who was feeling this connection between us. I could tell by the way her body reacted to my touch that she was just as caught up in this as I was. The problem was that *I* was the one who needed to say no and put an end to it, yet I couldn't. She was like a drug, and I found myself constantly waiting for my next hit.

I thanked my mom for everything and was getting ready to head out when she leaned against the kitchen counter and looked at me. I knew that look. I hated that look. It was the look that said we were about to have a conversation I wasn't going to like. I blew out a breath and sat down at the table, waiting for her to get on with it.

"What's up, mom?"

"I'm worried about you," she said quietly, studying

me as if I had some horrendous illness showing on my face.

"Why are you worried about me?" I asked, completely clueless.

"You're acting different lately. I can't put my finger on it, but something is definitely different about you."

"Nothing is different. I'm just busy with work, like always," I groaned and leaned back against the wooden chair. I already knew the lecture that was seconds away from coming out of her about how I'm always working too hard and how I don't enjoy life as much as I should.

"This isn't about you being busy," her voice trailed off as her features changed, the frown quickly replaced by a soft smile that played at her lips. It was as if something suddenly clicked inside her head, and she had the answer she was looking for. She smiled and touched her hand to her heart. "You're in love."

I pulled my head back, bewilderment splattered across my face.

"What?!" I exclaimed. "I think you're more tired than you're willing to admit because that's just crazy." I shook my head and felt myself getting irritated with the smile that was still plastered across her face.

"You can deny it if you want to," she said, pushing away from the counter as she wagged a finger in the air at me. "But I know you better than anyone, and you, my dear, are in love."

My mind immediately went to Eva, and I started to panic as I thought about how much control she had over me without even trying. She could ask for anything in the world, and I would find a way to give it to her. But to say that I was in love with her was absolutely ridiculous. We had barely known each other for a month, if you counted when we first met at the club—which I didn't. It wasn't like I had been trying to get to know her as I fucked her in the linen closet.

As I tried to justify that I couldn't be feeling anything close to love for her, I thought back to when I was in her apartment, taking care of her while she was sick. That wasn't love, though. That was just being a good boss. Or maybe even a good friend. Hell, it should be that I was being a good human being who was caring for another person when they needed it. That didn't mean that I was in love with her… did it?

I stayed silent while my mom filled a kettle with water and then set it on the stove while I tried to process what I felt about Eva. Maybe I liked her more than I was willing to admit, and that was why I couldn't stay away from her.

"So, I noticed that you have someone new working in Cora's office," my mom prodded, turning slightly to look at me over her shoulder. "What happened with Cora?"

"Ugh." I groaned and ran a hand through my hair. "You don't want to know."

"Oh, I'm sure I don't. But I asked anyway, and given your reaction, I know I am right. That also leads me to believe that it's the new girl working across the hall from you that has you acting this way."

I didn't have to ask what she meant by *this way*. It was clear as day in her sing-song tone as she said it.

"Eva," I replied with a heavy sigh. "Her name is Eva."

While I didn't want to get into the nitty-gritty details with my mother, I knew she wasn't going to stop until she got what she wanted from me. Telling her Eva's name wasn't much, but hopefully, it would keep her satisfied for a little while until I could get out of there and avoid her for a bit.

"That's right. I remember her telling me that when I

stopped by on Wednesday."

I nodded and felt my lips pull into a tight smile as I tapped my knuckles against the table.

"She seems nice," my mom said as she walked over and set a cup of tea down in front of me before taking a seat across the table. She lifted the cup to her lips and took a small sip as she waited for me to talk about her.

"She's very nice. And smart. And overqualified for the work she's doing there." I laughed, thinking about how I still had yet to find time to train her.

"So, what's the problem?" she asked.

"The problem is that I can't be with her, yet I can't stay away from her." My eyes lowered and focused on the cup of tea before I raised it and took a sip.

"Because you work together?"

"That for starters." I sighed. "A lot is happening right now, and I don't want to risk jeopardizing my career by doing something stupid."

We sat in silence for a few minutes while sipping our tea.

"You know, you're not like your father," she said suddenly, taking me by surprise.

I lifted my head and studied her, finding the hurt on her face that I had seen so much of when I was growing up. I reached over and gently squeezed her hand.

"I don't know about that," I blew out. "I'm currently in the middle of a sexual harassment lawsuit because I wasn't smart enough to say no to Cora when she wanted to have sex in the boardroom. After that, she later tried to blackmail me to get a promotion that she wasn't qualified for."

My mom shook her head and covered her face with her hands before looking at me.

"Ethan, Ethan, Ethan," she chided. "What am I going to do with you?"

I shrugged and felt myself smiling along with her as she let out a soft, light-hearted laugh.

"I don't know." I chuckled, enjoying the fact that she didn't berate me for something I had done. Maybe she knew I had done enough of that myself and wanted to spare me this time.

"Don't be so hard on yourself. So, you got yourself into a bad situation at work—you know what you do when that happens?"

"Grab some peanut butter and make s'mores?" I suggested, grinning at the memories of my grandma.

"It works every time." Her face lit up with happiness and I knew that she was having the same happy memories as me.

"But seriously," she continued. "You're a smart guy and you have an amazing legal team at work. I don't doubt that you'll find a way to work through this lawsuit. Own up to the mistakes you've made and learn from them. But at the end of the day, you're still not your dad. I would never judge you for the choices you make as a single man, Ethan. But I think that you owe it to yourself to stop and think about what you want from life and whether that includes someone special."

I swallowed hard, my throat suddenly dry. If only solving this problem was as easy as she made it sound.

Sixteen
Eva

"Hey, Brit," I grumbled as I stepped to the side, watching my step as I tried to avoid getting my heel caught in the crack between the uneven sidewalks outside of my apartment. This morning was already starting rough, and it definitely acted like the Monday that it was. "How was Miami?" I asked once I avoided the disaster and made my way toward the subway. I was already running late and prayed that there wouldn't be any further delays this morning.

"Miami was wonderful," she cooed, making me jealous that I hadn't been on a vacation in so long that I would probably need to pick up a copy of a how-to guide before attempting to take one. "But I feel terrible that everything apparently fell apart while I was gone."

Her tone changed, and I knew that she had already heard the gossip from Gabi.

"When did Gabi call?" I asked, my features scrunching on my face. She waited a minute before answering, and I knew that she was stalling so she didn't have to admit that they had already talked. While Brittany had been my best friend for as long as I could remember, she was also one of the biggest gossipers that I knew, aside from my sister. It just made sense that they would latch onto each other once they knew.

"Brit," I coaxed as I slid past a lost couple holding up a map of Manhattan while blocking the sidewalk.

"We talked this morning. And I have to say, I'm kinda hurt that you didn't call me yourself to tell me that you were so sick that your incredibly sexy boss—whom you've already fucked, I might add, had to come to take care of you."

"I didn't call you because I didn't want to ruin your trip by having you worried about me when there was nothing that you could do from Miami."

"You're still avoiding the part about your totally fuckable boss," she taunted. "You know, the one that you had sex with in the FILE ROOM AT YOUR WORK."

I considered pulling the phone away from my ear as her voice boomed through it but decided against it to spare those walking close by from having to hear about my sex life.

"I'm gonna kill Gabi," I muttered into the phone, instantly regretting telling my sisters about what had happened. I should have known that it would get back to Brittany before I could even talk to her.

"Well, you can fill me in on all of the juicy details later," she said cheerfully. "I was really just calling to see how you were doing this morning… you know, with the whole Jeremy thing."

I stopped in my tracks and froze. What the hell was she talking about?

"What *Jeremy thing*?" I asked, moving to the side so people could get past me.

The phone was so quiet that I pulled it away from

my ear and checked to make sure the call hadn't been disconnected.

"Brit, what Jeremy thing are you talking about?" I snarled, his name instantly making my blood boil.

"Shit. I thought she had already told you."

"Who had already told me what?"

My foot tapped anxiously on the cement as I waited while the blood pulsed in my ears as my blood pressure skyrocketed.

"Gabi was supposed to call you to tell you that Lance hired an attorney."

"Yeah, I know. He supposedly got one of the best in Manhattan. What's that have to do with—" My voice trailed off as it clicked and suddenly made sense.

"Fuck," I muttered, letting my head fall back in frustration.

"I'm so sorry. I thought you knew," Brit apologized. "I wasn't trying to ruin your day by bringing him up. I just wanted to make sure you were okay. Now I feel terrible. Is there anything—"

"I gotta go. I'll call you tonight," I interrupted, hanging up before she could object.

Brit was my best friend, so I knew she wasn't going to hold it against me for hanging up on her. I had more important things to deal with this morning.

Thirty minutes later, my blood was still boiling as I got off the train and walked the few blocks to work. I was standing outside the building, trying to force myself to go inside, when I looked across the street and saw the building where Jeremy's new law firm was located. Against my better judgment, I turned on my heel and marched over.

The inside of the building was nice but not nearly as extravagant as Ethan's. Large crystal chandeliers hung above the receptionist's desk that sat square between two sets of elevators. There was an extensive directory on the wall behind the young girl sitting at the desk, looking completely out of place as if she didn't belong there. I squinted my eyes, avoiding her as I looked for Jeremy's floor number.

"May I help you?" she asked, moving to the right to block my view. I narrowed my eyes and looked down at her, glaring at the fake smile she offered.

"I'm here to see Jeremy Rollings. What floor is he on?"

I noticed a faint rush of color flush across her cheeks before she lowered her head and checked the computer in front of her. Knowing Jeremy, he was probably fucking her too.

"Mr. Rollings is located on the seventeenth floor. It's the elevator on your right."

She turned her attention back to her computer as the phone rang and she answered it. I walked to the elevator and pressed the button, waiting impatiently for it to come back down. A few minutes later, I was standing in front of another desk, waiting for the older woman with gray hair and a frown painted on her face to hang up the phone and acknowledge me.

"Can I help you?" she said grumpily. I felt a low chuckle escape my lips as I thought about how Jeremy probably wasn't screwing this one and wondering if that's why she was hired in the first place. Remove all temptation and whatnot. While he had switched law firms after getting caught with his pants down, that didn't mean he had changed his ways.

"I need to see Jeremy Rollings," I said with as much

cheer as I could muster. If I was going to get past grumpy ass, I was going to need to fake my excitement to see Jeremy. My cheeks physically ached from the smile I was forcing them to carry.

"Do you have an appointment?"

I gritted my teeth as my frustration mounted. I didn't have the time nor the patience for this right now. I knew Lance had switched office buildings since the last time I'd visited him, so I had no idea where his office was in this building.

"Yes," I lied. "He's expecting me now, actually. So if you can please let him know that I'm here, I would really appreciate it."

"I don't see you on his schedule," she countered before looking over her shoulder to an office behind her.

"Well, I'm on it now," I said sarcastically as I rolled my eyes and walked past her, now knowing which office was his. I opened the door and stood there, staring at him as his eyes went wide with shock before shifting to pissed off.

"Hi. We need to talk." I tried to force a smile, but I knew it looked as strained as it felt. Being around Jeremy did nothing but raise my blood pressure, but I knew that if I had any chance of getting him to help me, I had to be nice.

"What the fuck are you doing, storming into my office unannounced?!" he demanded, standing up behind his desk. It had only been three months since he walked out and left me, and apparently, he had been using that time to hit the gym. I couldn't remember the last time that I had seen him in this good of shape nor did I remember his torso looking that defined under a dress shirt when we were together. While he had definitely made some improvements, he had nothing compared to Ethan. I shifted my weight, straightening my back as I tried to find my confidence.

"I was hoping to talk to you about you representing Lance," I replied, trying to keep myself calm and collected as I held my hands at my sides. "My family would appreciate it if you reconsidered taking him on as a client due to a conflict of interest, given our past."

"Who I take on as a client is none of your business, Eva," he growled. "*Nothing* I do is your business."

"It is when you're representing the asshole who's married to my sister!"

"You and I aren't together anymore. Therefore, I have no loyalties to you or your family. Lance is a client who is willing to pay whatever it takes to make sure he gets what he wants. It's as simple as that." He shrugged and let his hands fall to his sides.

It was a struggle to fight the urge to reach across and slap the stupid smirk off his face.

"You are such an asshole," I spit out, regretting that I had come here to begin with.

It was stupid to think there would be any chance of talking him out of representing Lance.

Before he could respond, I turned to leave and ran into a broad, chiseled chest. Strong hands reached out to grab me, holding me in place as my ankle twisted in the thin heel I was wearing. I slowly looked up and found concern on Ethan's face as he studied me before looking into Jeremy's office.

"Are you okay?" he asked quietly, his hands still on my waist.

"Yeah, I'm fine. Thanks." I could feel Jeremy's eyes on us as he stared.

"What's going on?" Ethan asked, loud enough for Jeremy to hear.

I watched as Jeremy walked over, standing too close to me for comfort. Ethan's hand curled possessively around my waist while he waited.

"This is Jeremy. My ex-fiancé," I said unenthusiastically. "He is representing my sister's abusive husband in a custody battle after she asked him for a divorce."

"And who exactly are you?" Jeremy asked, his eyes narrowed as he pulled his shoulders back in an attempt to look stronger than Ethan. He wasn't—not by a long shot.

"None of your fucking business," Ethan responded, his eyes shifting from Jeremy back to me. "Are you done here?"

"Yeah," I whispered so only he could hear as I continued to enjoy the comfort of his hands on me. As we turned to leave, I glanced over my shoulder one last time.

"Be sure to tell your sister that I look forward to seeing her soon," Jeremy said, his eyes darkening.

I could feel my body tense as I turned to go back into his office. Before I could take a step, Ethan's hand grabbed hold of my arm and led me down the hall and to the elevator. My blood pressure was sky-high, and my fingers trembled as the adrenaline shot through me. Once we were outside, Ethan walked me over to an empty bench and sat down while I paced back and forth. I closed my eyes and rolled my head back on my neck, trying to alleviate some of the tension. He didn't say anything as he allowed me some space to get myself together.

"I'm sorry about all of that," I mumbled, glancing quickly at him as I continued to pace in front of him.

"Don't be," he said coolly. He leaned back comfortably on the bench and rested his ankle on his knee as if he had all damn day to sit there. I hated that he had seen this side of me more than I hated that Jeremy was the dick I always knew he was. There was no loyalty where Jeremy was concerned—hence his cheating. I had no idea why I thought for a second that he would suddenly grow a conscience and agree to step away from taking Lance as a client.

"So, I'm gonna take a wild guess and say this is what had you so riled up during lunch last week?" Ethan questioned, his voice still calm as he extended his arm along the top of the bench.

"Yes and no. I've been stressed over my sister's situation in general, but I didn't know that Jeremy was the lawyer representing her husband until this morning. It was the final straw for me, I guess?" I scrunched my face, hating that I didn't know what to say at this point.

An awkward silence fell between us, quickly replaced by the hustle of people moving about, trying to get where they needed to go.

"Apparently, I didn't handle the news that well." I let out an awkward laugh and continued to pace. He didn't say anything. He just sat there watching me until I kept talking.

"My sister's husband is an asshole. She came to my apartment a few weeks ago with her face covered in bruises after he beat the shit out of her. It wasn't the first time, and I know it won't be the last time unless she goes through with getting a divorce. The problem is that they have a child together, my nephew, Jackson. He's only four, and he needs his mother." I could feel my voice crack as the tears started welling in my eyes. "She's my baby sister, and she works her ass off to take care of her son. She doesn't deserve what he's doing to her, and I know that she can't afford to hire a better lawyer. He's playing these games with her simply because he can. It kills me that I can't help her."

I blew out a deep breath and looked over at Ethan. He had a somber look on his face before he lowered his head and clasped his hands together, resting his elbows on his knees.

"I'm sorry. I didn't mean to drag you into all of this. I promise I'm fine now. We can head to the office, and I will make sure to keep all of my personal stuff out of my work day."

"You have nothing to apologize for, Eva," he assured me as he got up and stood in front of me. "I know first-hand how hard it is to get caught up in a nasty custody battle." He paused for a minute, then ran a hand through his hair. "Who's your sister's lawyer?"

"Some guy she found online." I sighed heavily as a frustrated chuckle slipped past my lips. "He was the cheapest, and she refused to let me help her pay for a better one. Jeremy is as ruthless as her husband. I'm terrified that this will end badly, and she'll lose custody of her son because Lance can buy whatever outcome he wants. And the really shitty thing is that he doesn't even want full custody—he barely spends time with him as it is. He would only be doing this to spite her because he can."

"I know a guy. I'll give you his info when we get back to the office."

"Is he any good?" I asked cautiously. I knew that if Ethan was referring someone, they had to be good. What I really wanted to ask was how much this guy was going to cost us. I made good money, but that didn't mean I would be able to spend all of it on a lawyer for my sister.

"He's the best," Ethan replied, tilting his head to the side. "And he owes me a favor, so let your sister know that she can get rid of the other guy and save that money for something else."

"Ethan, you don't have to do that." My face fell as I thought about how pathetic I must have looked for him to offer something like that to help my family. I didn't want nor need his pity. "Thank you, but I'll look into things, and we'll figure out a way to pay for his services. I appreciate you getting me his information."

"I know I don't have to," he said softly, turning and gently grabbing my elbow to lead me to the office. "I want to."

We walked in silence for a few minutes, my anger finally starting to subside. As we waited for the elevator up to our offices, I realized that I had no idea why he was even at Jeremy's work to begin with.

"What were you doing at Hyde and Wilson this morning anyway?" I asked as the bell dinged and we stepped inside the elevator.

"I was meeting with a lawyer that Brent asked me to speak to. He's working through his estate and his own custody issues with Karly and wanted to make sure that I spoke with his lawyer about the deal with Watson Investments."

"Have you heard any more about what he wants to do with that deal?" I asked, realizing that I hadn't heard any updates from him on what was happening.

"Nope. Right now he's spending time with Chloe, and apparently, there's a new woman in his life that he's been seeing. We're supposed to meet next week to talk about things."

"Well, let me know if you need my help on any of it," I offered as the elevator doors opened and we stepped out. "Thank you for your support today. I really appreciate it." I smiled and lowered my head as I turned to head into my office.

"Not a problem. I'll get that information to you in a few minutes. Let me know if she has any trouble, but working with Art should make things a whole lot easier for her from here on out."

I smiled and nodded before walking into my office and sitting down behind my desk. Today was already turning out to be a crazy day, and it was barely nine o'clock in the morning.

<u>Seventeen</u>
Ethan

The day flew by faster than I had expected, and I was feeling the pain of being late to the office this morning. I had missed several important phone calls, and I had Garrett breathing down my neck for the report I had told him I would have over to his secretary by noon. Needless to say, I had yet to get that done either.

I hadn't expected to run into Eva this morning, especially at Hyde and Wilson, of all places. While I had been there to meet with the lawyer Brent had asked me to check in with, I was also there to meet with their Director of Human Resources. I hadn't told Regina or Garrett about the meeting and knew that they would try to talk me out of going. But when I found out that Cora had filed another sexual harassment lawsuit against another lawyer at their firm, I couldn't stay away. I needed to know what happened. There was a lot at risk with the lawsuit she had filed against me. Most importantly, I was afraid of the impact it might have on my relationship with Eva when she found out what I was being accused of.

It was almost two when my stomach started growling, making me realize that I had forgotten to eat today. Kate had checked in briefly earlier to see if I needed her to order food, but I had been distracted and shooed her away before I stopped to think about it. I glanced across the hall to Eva's office and noticed the granola bar on her desk. From the looks of it, she hadn't eaten yet, either.

On the computer, I opened an instant message box and typed in her name, waiting for the chat box to load. There was this sudden feeling of giddiness running through me as I watched her, waiting to see when she got the pop-up notification of a new chat message from me.

Me: Have you eaten lunch yet?

My fingers hovered over the keyboard, waiting for her response. From the corner of my eye, I saw her look over at me, but I didn't turn to look at her. Instead, I kept my focus on my computer screen and pretended like I was busy. A smile played on my lips when I watched her turn her attention back to the computer, her hands typing. She uncrossed her legs and shifted slightly in her chair before crossing them again. I loved that her desk was open at the bottom, which allowed me to see her beautiful legs during the day when she was sitting at her computer.

Eva: I had a granola bar. You?

I thought about replying with the truth—that I desperately wanted to crawl under her desk and eat her. But I didn't.

Me: Got too busy. Completely spaced it.

I watched as the dots appeared in the chat box as she typed her response.

Eva: You do seem a little distracted today. Sorry if I contributed to that this morning.

I tapped my fingers on the keyboard, debating what to reply with.

Me: Distracted would be an understatement.

Eva: Why? What's happening? Can I help?

Me: I can't seem to keep my eyes off of your sexy legs every time you uncross them.

I waited for a few seconds to see what she was going to say when I felt her eyes on me. I turned my head slightly, feeling the heat of her gaze from across the hall. I reached up and loosened my tie as the temperature in the room suddenly rose. Eva pushed her chair back and looked down before glancing at me one last time. She pulled herself back to her computer and fucking uncrossed her legs again, painfully slow this time.

Eva: I wasn't aware that you could see under my desk. My apologies.

I felt a low chuckle rumble out of me.

Me: I should be the one to apologize for wishing that there was more to see.

This time, she didn't turn to look at me as the dots started bouncing in the chat bubble as she typed.

Eva: What exactly would you like to see?

I didn't waste any time responding.

Me: Your beautiful pussy.

I glanced over and watched the blush that crept up her neck to her cheeks. I was thankful that she chose to wear her hair up so I could see the way her body reacted to me. I was even more thankful that she had decided to wear a short, silky black skirt with thin black heels. She turned slightly in her chair to face me, her eyes quickly shifting to look down the hall. I had no idea what she was planning to do, but it was the middle of the day, and Kate was sitting right down the hallway at her desk.

Eva: I don't think this solves your lunch dilemma,

but here you go.

She slowly spread her legs open, bracing her feet to the side in a position that lifted her skirt enough to give me a view of the thin black thong that was covering her.

Me: That's a fucking sexy view, but it would be even better without the panties.

I knew the moment that the chat was received in her office by the expression on her face. She lifted her finger to her lip and bit it before standing up and walking over to the side of her office that was out of view. A few seconds later, she came back and sat down before opening the drawer beside her. She glanced at me briefly before closing it and returning her attention to her computer.

There were no dots bouncing, indicating that she was typing a response and I felt myself starting to worry that I had crossed the line.

Suddenly, she slowly turned her chair, facing me again. She looked up and locked eyes with me as she uncrossed her legs and spread them, showing me her beautiful, perfectly waxed pussy. I swallowed hard, fighting the urge to storm over and close her door before fucking her on her desk.

She leaned back in her chair, legs still spread, as she slid the keyboard in front of her. Her eyes stayed glued to me for a few seconds before she looked away and typed something.

Eva: Happy?

Was I happy? Fuck yeah, I was happy. And horny. And a bunch of other things that you could probably use to describe the seven dwarves of erotica. But I wanted more.

Me: Happy. Horny. My balls are bluer than the sky.

Me: I would rather be in front of you, on my knees, tasting you.

Eva: I wouldn't complain about that, but I think we need to discuss proper nutrition if you think this is lunch.

Me: I could eat you for breakfast, lunch, and dinner.

Eva: Promises, promises.

Me: Trust me, baby, I can deliver.

I felt the pressure as my dick strained against my trousers, desperate for a release.

Eva: Is that so?

Me: I don't recall you having any complaints from the three times I've fucked you already.

Eva: True, but you've yet to go down on me. Just saying there could be room for disappointment…

Me: Do you remember how good my tongue felt as it ran across your neck when I fucked you from behind in the closet at the club?

Eva: Yes. I remember it frequently…

Me: Imagine that I'm running my tongue along your slit, slowly licking every inch of your pussy.

Eva: Imagination isn't the same…

Me: Okay. Fair enough.

Me: Let's do a quick little test, shall we?

Eva: What is it?

Me: I bet that I can make you come without even

touching you.

Eva: I seriously doubt it.

Me: Deal or no deal, Eva.

Eva: Fine… Deal.

I rubbed my hands together as the excitement pooled through me.

Me: You have to do exactly as I say—got it?

Eva: Got it.

Me: Don't sound so enthused.

Eva: I just know you're going to lose, and I already feel bad for you.

I let a laugh slip out as I looked across the hallway and stared at her. She looked over, a smug smile on her face as I raised an eyebrow at her. She had no idea who she was playing with. Game. On.

Me: Take your finger and slowly touch yourself.

I watched as she read the words, her body stiffening in response.

Me: Now, Eva. Slide a finger inside of your pussy.

Her shoulders rose and fell as she let out a long breath before casting a glance at me. Her hand slowly moved under her desk and brushed against her thigh before it hesitated by her pussy. I could see how nervous she was that I was watching her, and it turned me on even more. She closed her eyes and leaned her head back against the leather chair, spreading her legs open even more to slide a finger along her slit. My dick twitched as I watched her body react to the sensation of her touch, knowing that she was fully aroused.

Me: Good, now stick another finger inside.

Her eyes flickered open as she read the message. She didn't bother looking my way before doing as I asked and slid another finger inside. My eyes were fixated on her hand as she fingered herself under her desk while I watched.

Me: Now, tell me how wet you are.

She kept her fingers inside, working them in and out of her pussy while she reached over and typed with the other hand.

Eva: So wet…

Me: Good. I can't wait to see your face as you come for me in a few minutes.

Eva: We'll see.

Me: Take your finger and slide it up to your clit. Rub those juices all over it.

I leaned back in my chair, thankful that my desk was fully covered in the front so no one could see as I unzipped my pants and pulled my dick out. It was hard as a fucking rock, my hand working up and down the shaft as I watched her rub her clit. I continued to stroke myself with my left hand so I could type with my right.

Me: Rub it harder, Eva. Rub it as you think about how hard my dick was as I plowed into you from behind against this window.

My orgasm was close, the pressure building as I watched her and thought back to us fucking in my office. Her eyes were trying to stay open so she could read the messages, but I could tell her orgasm was close as well by how she was straining to focus and pay attention.

Me: Rub it for me and imagine the guy who was jacking off while watching us fuck. I bet he wished he

could be in front of you while you took his big dick down your throat and I fucked you from behind.

Her eyes closed after she read the words I had sent, her fingers rubbing her clit quickly while her other hand roamed up her body and caressed her breast. I watched the way her body shifted, and her hips bucked as she lifted off the chair, her orgasm ripping through her while she tried to stifle a moan. Her face looked beautiful, her lips parted, and her mouth opened as she came undone in her office. I closed my eyes as I came under my desk, gripping the edge of it tightly while my other hand finished me off.

Me: Told you.

I leaned back against my chair as my breathing started to even out. I had a mess to clean up, but thankfully, there was a bathroom attached to my office, and no one would notice if I changed pants, given I typically wore black slacks.

Eva: It was worth it…

Me: I've never been so jealous of your fingers as I am right now. Lick them and tell me how good you taste.

Eva: Come over here and do it yourself. Unless you're afraid you won't be able to control yourself…

Me: I think we both know that the whole office will know that we're fucking if I come over there and lick your fingers, Eva. There is no control when it comes to you.

I hadn't meant to say that to her, but when she looked at me with longing on her face, I knew she already knew. We were damned either way.

****

Eva and I avoided each other for the rest of the day with neither of us bothering to stop and actually eat lunch.

By the time I had a few minutes free to eat something, it was already time to head home. I walked out of my office at the same time as Eva and noticed her cheeks flush with color as she lowered her head and tried to avoid looking at me. I struggled to keep the smile off my face but found it nearly impossible as I replayed the images of what had happened earlier.

We stood in the hallway, waiting for the other to go first but neither of us bothered to move. Finally, I said, "Hey, about earlier—"

"Don't worry about it," she said, sticking her hand up to stop me.

"I don't want you to be embarrassed about it."

"I'm not," she lied as she laughed nervously. "Okay, I am. But not as much as I thought I would be." She gave a little shrug as she held her purse down in front of her and kept her head lowered.

"Well, that's good to know." I chuckled, feeling relieved that this wasn't as awkward as it could be. The last thing I wanted to do was make her feel uncomfortable or embarrassed about what happened. Hell, if I had my way, I would have shut the entire office down for the day so I could have pleasured her the way I wanted to under her desk.

"I'm starting to think that you're a bad influence on me," she teased as we started walking down the hallway to the main elevators. I glanced at Kate's desk and noticed that she was already gone for the day.

"It's only a bad influence if it has a negative impact," I said matter-of-factly. "But given how relaxed you look, I would say there was no negative impact."

"What am I going to do with you?" She sighed playfully, stopping suddenly when we walked into the lobby.

A woman was standing by the wall with her back turned toward us. I didn't know if anyone had helped her yet, and it seemed unlikely that anyone would be expecting a client this late in the day. I was about to ask if I could help her when she turned around and ran a hand over her swollen stomach, an evil grin on her face as she watched my reaction.

"Cora?" I asked in disbelief. "What are you doing here?"

"I think we need to talk," she said, rubbing her bump. "Privately."

Her tone was sharp as her eyes cut to Eva.

Eighteen
Eva

The tension that surrounded us was thick in the air as Ethan glared at the beautiful, *very* pregnant woman in front of us.

"I should go," I said quietly, lowering my head and looking away as I started to walk off. Whatever this was, it didn't look like it needed me to stick around and be involved. I had no idea who she was or what their history was, but the evil glare she was sending my way made me well aware that my presence wasn't wanted.

"No," he said sharply, grabbing hold of my elbow to stop me. "You can stay. Cora is leaving."

"I'm not leaving until we talk." She put her hand on her hip and narrowed her eyes at him.

"Anything you have to say, you can say to my attorney. We will not be having any private meetings, and it's absurd that you would think that I would even consider it."

"Things have changed," she bit out angrily. "And we need to discuss those changes and your responsibility with them."

"Cora, as I've said—you will speak directly with my lawyer—end of story. I don't know who let you in, but you don't work here anymore. Given our situation, you need to leave. Now."

"Why? Are you fucking *her* now? Is that why you are so eager to get rid of me?" Cora snapped and turned her attention to me. "He might be fun to look at, and he's a great fuck, but be careful, or you'll end up in the same sort of mess as me. Knocked up by a man who tries to pay her off, so she'll go away instead of doing the right thing."

I felt my stomach drop as I looked at Ethan. His jaw was clenched, face etched in anger. But he didn't bother to deny it. I looked between the two of them and wondered if there was any truth in what she was saying. I was also curious about their situation and why Ethan had a lawyer involved. Suddenly, I had so many questions but didn't feel like I was in a position to ask them. If he wanted me to know his business, he would have told me.

It was awkward and uncomfortable standing there, waiting for someone to say something as Cora's gut-punching words lingered in the air. I wanted to leave, but Ethan's grip on my elbow told me that he wanted me to stay. *Needed* me to stay.

After what felt like a few minutes, Cora huffed dramatically before turning around and leaving. I waited until she was in the elevator and the door closed before I turned to look at Ethan.

My words were so jumbled in my head that I couldn't get a coherent sentence out if I tried. Instead, I just stared at him as I silently bombarded him with a million questions. His eyes softened as he ran a hand through his hair.

"I'm sorry about that," he started, stalling as he thought about what to say as well. "Cora was a former employee who—"

"Did you sleep with her?" I blurted out, feeling the need to know if she was telling the truth.

He closed his eyes and pinched the bridge of his nose.

"Yes."

"When she worked for you?"

"Yes."

"Were you guys a couple?"

"No."

My heart started to race when I realized where my questions were going and how much I was dreading the next answer.

"Were you just fucking her like you're just fucking me?"

He blew out a heavy breath and looked at me without answering. I could feel the anxiety flowing, pulsing through me as I waited. I raised an eyebrow at him and tilted my head, needing an answer.

"I wouldn't say it that way," he said softly, guilt plastered across his face.

"That's all I needed to know," I replied hastily as I turned and walked away. I could hear his footsteps right behind me as he followed.

"Eva, stop," he pleaded as I kept walking.

I went past the elevators and swung open the door to the stairs, feeling too angry to wait. I needed to get away from him and put some distance between us.

"Can we please talk about this?" He grabbed my arm to stop me. I swung around to face him, our bodies only inches apart.

"Is what she said about you trying to pay her to walk away true?" I asked, stopping briefly to let him answer. My ears flushed as my blood pressure skyrocketed.

"It's not what it sounds like."

I pulled in a deep breath and leaned against the wall behind me as I tried to gather my thoughts.

"You know, when I was with Jeremy, there were so many times that I would question something he had said or done. And every single time, he would respond with *it's not what it looks like* or *it's not what it sounds like*. The problem was that I believed him. I second-guessed myself so often that I ended up forcing myself to believe what he was telling me. Even when I caught him fucking his secretary on his desk one night when he was supposed to be working late. Do you know what he said to me? It's not what it looks like."

I folded my arms over my chest as I tapped my foot angrily while I watched Ethan's face as he listened.

"I've learned that when people say something isn't what it seems—they're usually lying. It is *exactly* what it seems. So I'm sorry if I don't believe you when you say that whatever is going on with that woman isn't what it sounds like. In fact, it's none of my business. You've made it crystal clear that you're not a relationship kind of guy, and now I see why."

I shook my head as I turned and walked down the stairs, somewhat relieved and even more disappointed when he didn't follow.

Nineteen
Ethan

I'd spent Tuesday morning in a closed-door meeting with Regina and Garrett as I gave them the update on Cora's surprise visit. Garrett was looking into options for requesting a paternity test while I tried to do the math to see if there was any fucking way that I could be the father, to begin with. The more we talked about the situation, the more I wished that I would have just given in and paid her off when she first demanded it. Not that it would have earned me any bonus points with Eva. If anything, it would have been the final nail in the coffin of our non-existent relationship.

I figured it was also best to disclose my meeting yesterday at Hyde and Wilson before they somehow found out on their own. Regina was going to reach out to their Director of Human Resources to see if our legal team could set up a meeting with theirs to discuss a course of action. Granted, there was little that either side could talk about at this point, but it was good to know what resources we had if we needed them.

Regina excused herself to make a quick phone call, leaving Garrett and me alone in the boardroom.

"How's Eva working out?" Garrett asked, trying to

break the silence that had filled the room.

"Honestly, I don't know. I haven't had much time to sit down and work with her, and she was out of the office for a little while when she got sick. Regina and Kate have helped her get set up on a few things, but overall, she seems like she's just teaching herself the ropes."

"I'm sure things will level out soon," he assured me as he held his pen between his two index fingers and looked at it. "Aside from the work stuff, how are things with Eva?"

I looked up at him, wondering how he knew anything had happened between us.

"Mom told me you were in love. I just assumed it was with her since your productivity has gone to shit since she started working here," he replied with a laugh, noticing the confused look I had on my face when he asked.

"Of course she did." I rolled my eyes and turned my attention back to my brother, who had a shit-eating grin on his face. "What's so damn funny?" I asked, feeling my lips turning up into a smile.

"Nothing, I just never thought I would see the day."

"When I fell in love or when I started slacking at work?" I teased.

"Both." He pulled his head back and laughed, setting the pen down on the table.

"It's not all it's cracked up to be. Now I see why some men stay bachelors their entire life."

"Relationships take time and hard work. There's no way around that. But when you find the right person, it no longer feels like work. You end up going out of your way to do things to make the other person happy, and sometimes, it means temporarily sacrificing your own happiness."

"That sounds terrible," I joked, trying to keep from acknowledging that I knew exactly what he was talking about because that was what I wanted to do for Eva.

"You joke about it now, but when you're tossing and turning at night because you can't sleep and can't eat—it won't be so funny then."

"I think my DNA is missing whatever gene is responsible for all of that. Apparently, you got yours from mom, and I inherited all the terrible traits from dad."

I saw the anger flash across Garrett's face and almost immediately regretted bringing our dad up. It wasn't an easy subject for either of us to talk about, but he always flew off the handle first. I waited for him to go into a long lecture about what a terrible person our father was for cheating on our mom, but he didn't. For the first time, he stayed calm and didn't react to it.

"You're nothing like dad."

His words stunned me as I looked at him, waiting for him to take them back.

"Seriously, Ethan. You're nothing like him." He shook his head and looked out the window. "Dad was selfish and never bothered to worry about making anyone happy other than himself. He constantly cheated on Mom, and when she would call him on his bullshit, he would apologize and beg her for another chance. When that stopped working, he started manipulating her and threatened to take us away from her. You know Mom would do anything for her boys. Even if that meant staying married to him longer than she should have."

I felt the nausea rise as I thought back to my childhood and the fights that I remembered my parents having. The constant yelling and screaming. The look of pain on my mom's face when she would look at me before she went running off to make amends with my dad. I always thought that maybe she wasn't strong enough to leave him. Now, I understood that she was strong enough to stay with a man that she didn't love so that she could do what she thought was best for her children.

"Our legal team will handle the shit with Cora, and we'll get a paternity test. Right now, there's nothing that you need to do. As far as things with Eva are concerned, if you love her, you should tell her. Find a way to get out of your head and make this work."

"It's not that easy," I replied, remembering the look on her face when she stormed off last night.

"Why not?"

"Because she's pissed off at me, for one."

He raised his eyebrows, questioning what I had done this time.

"She was here with me last night when Cora showed up. I hadn't told her about Cora or the lawsuit because I thought it was best *not* to talk about it. All Eva saw was that some woman showed up, claiming to be pregnant with my child and accusing me of trying to pay her off instead of doing the right thing. Given that Eva and I didn't have a relationship outside of work, I can't blame her for feeling like she's being treated the same way Cora was."

"Shit."

"Yep. And on top of that, we had just talked about how her sister's husband hired Eva's ex-fiancé to represent him in a custody battle. The same fiancé who was constantly cheating on Eva."

"Well, dear brother, that's some mess you've got."

I leaned back in my chair and laughed.

"Really, that's all you've got? Where's your brotherly

advice when I need it?" I threw my hands up as I tried to play the part of being devasted by his lack of compassion, but the smile gave me away.

"That's the funny thing about love. No one can give you advice on it. You're the only person who knows what she means to you and what you're willing to do for her." He sighed softly as he adjusted his tie. "But I will say one thing…"

"What's that?" I chuckled, knowing that he couldn't ever walk away without getting the last word in.

"Don't be so afraid of falling in love that you stop it from happening. You deserve to be happy."

He stood up and checked his watch. "Sorry to leave you in this mess you've created for yourself, but I have to run. I've got a meeting in thirty minutes," he said.

I glanced at my phone, mainly to see if Eva had texted or called. Nothing. I had a meeting with Brent in an hour, and I needed to get my head straight before he got there. I gathered my stuff and stood up.

"Thanks for the talk," I said warmly, reaching out to shake his hand as we reached the door. He grabbed mine and pulled me in for a hug instead.

I couldn't remember the last time Garrett had hugged me, but I wasn't about to question it now. Not when everything in my life seemed to be changing at once, and there was only one person I could think of who was to blame. Eva.

Twenty
Eva

"I don't know much about him. Ethan said that he's one of the best family law attorneys in Manhattan, and he owes him a favor," I said, trying to hold my phone in between my ear and shoulder while I folded the laundry that was scattered across my bed. I was good at getting my work attire hung right away so it didn't wrinkle, but the clothes I wore to go running were a whole different story.

"That's really nice of him to do that," Lucy replied, and I could hear the hesitation in her voice.

I sighed and set the pair of yoga pants that I was about to fold on the bed. I reached up and held the phone, giving my neck a break from the uncomfortable position it had been in.

"What's wrong? Why do you sound so unsure about this?" I asked.

"It's nothing. I'm sure he's a great attorney."

"But…" I pressed.

"But there has to be a catch. Men aren't nice to women for no reason, Eva. You know that as well as I do."

I let my mind wander for a minute, thinking about Ethan and how I really did think he was a great guy until I found out about Cora. While it was childish of me to judge him for something that I didn't know anything about, I couldn't help but feel betrayed that he hadn't bothered to tell me. Things had moved so quickly between us, and there was constantly this gray area that made it hard to know where we stood. The only thing certain was that we were coworkers who had slept together several times. Other than that, I wasn't sure if we were even friends outside of work or if there was a possibility that our fucking would lead to something more.

"Ethan was very sympathetic with what you're going through, and honestly, I think he offered to help more because of his first impression of Jeremy."

She was quiet on the other line for a few minutes, pausing to tell Jackson to finish his dinner before she came back.

"So, are you guys officially seeing each other now? Was he jealous of Jeremy, and that's what made him want to help?"

"We're not seeing each other. Things are just…" I sighed heavily.

"Complicated?" she offered.

"How did you know?"

"Things are always complicated with you," she replied with a laugh.

"Gee, thanks," I said sarcastically.

"I don't mean that in a bad way. I'm sorry. I just meant that you don't let your guard down easily, so it tends to make things more complicated than they are."

"No, trust me—with Ethan, things are definitely

complicated, and it's not because of me. He constantly flirts with me, and then there's the office sex that we can't seem to stop having. But outside of work, I don't hear anything from him. Add in the former employee who recently showed up at the office, *pregnant* and claiming that he tried to pay her off so she would leave him alone and things are *super* complicated."

"Did you ask him about her and if the baby was his? Why would he pay her to leave him alone?"

"I asked him if she was telling the truth, and he said that it wasn't what it looked like or some stupid shit like that."

"And?"

"And I walked away. I'm tired of the whole *it's not what it looks like* game. I'm almost forty and don't have the time or patience for these games. I left those behind with—"

"Jeremy," she finished for me.

"Exactly."

"But Eva, don't you think you owe it to Ethan to allow him to explain what happened? If you guys aren't in a relationship, then it might have been hard for him to open up and talk to you about it. You forget that not many guys like to talk about past relationships or whatever she might have been. Even fewer are willing to do it with a girl they're not *technically* dating. And you're failing to realize the most important thing here."

"And what's that?"

"That he's *not* Jeremy. You're punishing him for what your ex did to you instead of giving him a chance to tell you what really happened."

"I've given him the opportunity to talk to me about it, and he hasn't bothered." I tilted my chin up, even though she couldn't see me.

"Have you, though?" I could hear the judgmental tone in her voice.

I stalled, trying to answer her as I struggled to find a way to prove that I was right. The problem was that I hadn't allowed him to talk to me after I walked out Monday night. Tuesday, he had been in meetings all day, and when his afternoon appointment with Brent got rescheduled, I closed my door and pretended that I was on a phone call to avoid him. I had been acting childish all along and couldn't keep blaming him for not talking to me about what happened.

"Well, I know that the silence means that you know that I'm right. I'm gonna let you go so I can throw Jackson in a bath before bed," she said with a hint of sarcasm. "I'll call the lawyer in the morning and let you know how it goes, but I doubt I'll get to meet with him this week since tomorrow is already Thursday."

"Sounds good. Please keep me posted."

"I will," she assured me. "Oh, I almost forgot. Gabi wanted to see about getting together for a few drinks Friday night. Are you free?"

"I'll have to check my schedule and get back to you," I joked. She knew I didn't have a life on Friday nights.

"I'm sure you can catch up on your TV shows on Saturday," she teased.

"Hey, I could have plans on Saturday, too. You never know."

"Yes, as long as they end by four so you can have an early supper…"

I could hear her laughing on the other end as she pulled the phone away to try to hide it.

"You're such a little shit. I'll talk to you tomorrow. Go give my stinky nephew a bath."

"Ugh," she groaned. "He is stinky."

"I was kidding."

"I'm not. I swear, no matter how clean I get him, he finds a way to undo it within minutes. But anyways, I will talk to you tomorrow."

"Sounds good. I love you."

"Love you too."

I was reluctant to admit it, but I felt better after talking to my sister. Probably because I knew she was right; I just hadn't wanted to admit it before now. I folded the rest of the laundry and put it away. It was still early, and I was tired of eating takeout, so I grabbed my keys to run out to buy some groceries. And by groceries, I meant frozen pizza and wine.

Twenty-One
Ethan

"What is that smell?" I asked Kate as I stopped at her desk and sniffed the air. It smelled like something was on fire.

"Um, toast," she said quietly, glancing down the short hallway to Eva's office. "Ms. Sanchez made toast this morning."

I pulled my lips in, forcing myself to hold the laughter in. I tapped my knuckles against the top of Kate's desk a few times and smiled before I walked down the hall. I was surprised that the fire alarm wasn't going off, given that the closer I got to her office, the worse the smell was.

I stood outside her door and knocked lightly on it, pulling her attention away from the computer. On a plate beside her keyboard were two pieces of black toast.

"Morning," I said as she looked up at me and then glanced down at the toast nervously.

"Good morning," she said quietly. "I'm sorry about the smell, I made—"

"Toast," I finished for her. "I thought I smelled your culinary skills from the elevator."

She grimaced and looked down again at the burnt disaster in front of her.

"Is that your breakfast?" I nodded to it.

"Yeah. But I'll probably save myself the embarrassment and just eat a granola bar. I think I still have one or two in my desk." She pulled open the drawer to check and frowned when she couldn't find any. "I guess there goes that option as well."

I felt bad that I kept forgetting to replenish her stock from the one I swiped last week. It was on my to-do list with a million other things.

"How about we go to breakfast? I needed to talk to you this morning anyway. The least I can do is buy you something edible to eat."

"Don't you have meetings?" she asked. I could tell that she was hesitant to go.

"My first meeting isn't until ten-thirty, and it's with Brent. I wanted to talk with you about the Watson deal before he gets here. Plus, I owe you a granola bar, so until I can get you one, we'll have to make do with actual breakfast."

I waited for a minute as she sat there, staring at me without making any effort to get up. Shit, I must've pissed her off more than I thought.

"I'm not leaving until we go eat, and I'm starving, so…" I raised my eyebrows at her and shoved my hands into my pockets. She narrowed her eyes at me as she reached down, pulled her purse out of the drawer, and then stood up.

"Why do you owe me a granola bar?" she asked as she walked around the desk and stood next to me at the door.

"I might have stolen one while you were out sick." I rocked back on my heels and smiled, hoping she would find it cute and that it wouldn't piss her off even further.

After a minute, she pursed her lips and tilted her head to look up at me.

"I knew one was missing… and just for that, I'm ordering a side of pancakes with breakfast." She turned and walked out of her office, swinging her purse up onto her shoulder as her ass swayed perfectly behind her.

I shook my head and laughed. We walked a few blocks to the diner on the corner and found a booth in the back. It was busy for a Thursday morning, and I needed to be able to talk to her without having to shout over everyone else. While I needed to talk to her about Brent, I really wanted to clear the air between us about Cora.

"Do you know what you want?" I asked, looking over the top of my menu to see her.

"Everything looks delicious," she said as she looked at hers. "But I think I know what I'm getting."

At that moment, the waitress came back and set our cups of coffee on the table before pulling out her notepad to take our order.

"What can I get you guys?" she asked, looking between us. I nodded to Eva, and she turned to her and waited.

"I'll do the meat-lover skillet, but can I add onions and mushrooms?"

"Of course. Do you want toast or an English muffin?"

I felt Eva's eyes dart to mine with a warning look for me not to say anything.

"I'll have toast, please. On white bread. And a side of pancakes."

"You got it," she said before turning to me.

"I'll do the same," I replied, sliding my menu over next to Eva's. The waitress grabbed both menus from the table and rushed off to put our order in.

"Trying something new?" I asked, fighting to keep my tone serious.

"What do you mean?" She frowned, clearly missing where I was going with the question.

"White toast?"

Her face pulled up into the cutest angry face I had ever seen.

"Ha, ha. Real funny," she mocked as she wadded up a piece of her napkin and threw it at me. I ducked to the side, missing it before it hit the man behind me in the back of the head. He turned around and glared at us as he touched the spot where it had hit him. She clasped her hands over her mouth, and her eyes went wide in embarrassment.

"I'm so sorry about that, sir," I offered, turning to the side to see him better. "However, I am a lawyer, so if you'd like to discuss damages or seek legal counsel, I would be willing to help—free of charge." I winked playfully, only to receive an eye roll from him as he muttered under his breath about stupid kids before returning to his breakfast.

"You're gonna get us kicked out of here," I playfully warned, leaning closer to her across the table. "You better stop, or you'll never know what white toast tastes like." I leaned back and laughed, watching her shake her head at me.

"I've had real toast before," she countered. "I just happen to burn it more often these days. Maybe there's something wrong with the toaster in my office?"

I stopped and stared at her.

"What?" she exclaimed, throwing her hands up in the air. "Maybe it's not all *my* fault, maybe you have a faulty toaster… you know, *I* could seek legal counsel for that…"

"You found the toaster in your office?"

"Yeah," she replied cautiously. "Why do I get the feeling you're going to tell me something bad about it?"

I leaned my head back and laughed, trying to hide it behind the palm of my hand.

"You are the only person I know who would have the unfortunate fate of finding that fucking toaster." I laughed even harder.

"Why? What's wrong with it?" I could hear the slightest bit of panic in her voice. "Ethan! What's wrong with the toaster?"

I waited a few minutes for my laughter to subside before I answered her.

"Nothing is wrong with it, other than that thing has been an omen of bad luck since I was a kid. It was the first gift that my grandma bought Garrett when he went off to college. He hated it and never used it, but because it was from my grandma, he kept it. When he started Roberts and Associates, he brought it with him and would have it out in his office when she would stop by. I don't think that it has ever been used in all the years he's had it, and honestly, I'm sure he finally just tossed it in one of the offices until it got shuffled around and made it to yours."

"Well, then, I'm glad I yanked the plug out of the wall before it caught on fire," she admitted.

"You did what?" Suddenly, the humor was gone.

"Yeah, it was smoking really bad, and I was worried that it was going to catch on fire. I tried pushing the lever to pop the toast back out, but it didn't work, so I just pulled the plug out before it could catch on fire.”

I covered my face with my hands for a few seconds before looking at her.

“Promise me one thing?”

“What’s that?” she asked.

“Please don’t go near a toaster again for the rest of your life.”

She opened her mouth to say something at the same time the waitress came back with our food. She set everything down on the table in front of us and made sure we didn’t need anything before she walked off.

We were quiet for a few minutes while we ate, and neither of us bothered to stop to make small talk. The longer we went with the silence between us, the more I felt the pressure to talk to her about Cora. I waited until she had taken a bite before I started talking, hoping that it would be a good way for me to get out what I needed to say without any interruptions.

“I want to talk about what happened the other night,” I said abruptly. She looked up at me with an uneasiness on her face as she chewed the bite of pancakes she had just taken.

“I’m not going to get into the full details of what happened—mainly because I can’t, but also, I don’t imagine that you would care to hear them. However, Cora was a former employee of mine, and one night, while we were working late, we had sex.” I gulped and tried to ignore the hurt look that just flashed across her face.

“I wasn’t interested in a relationship, and I didn’t think she was either. Right after it happened, she started asking me for a promotion to a position that she wasn’t qualified for. When I told her no, she got upset and started making it hard for us to work together. I knew then that she wasn't interested in a relationship. She simply wanted the promotion. To fix the problem, I asked Regina to transfer her to another department with a slight pay increase. She refused the position and became a nuisance. We relieved her of her position, and at my recommendation, we gave her a severance package."

I paused for a moment to gather my thoughts as I tried to push the anger away.

"This all happened five months ago. I hadn't heard anything from her until a few weeks ago when I received the paperwork that she had filed a sexual harassment lawsuit against me. Our legal team has been handling everything, and I haven't had any contact with her. Regina insisted that from here on out, I don't take any meetings with female clients or employees unless I have you in the room with me," I explained. "That's why I didn't want you to leave when she was there. I needed you to be there as my witness that nothing happened in case she decided to add more to her false accusations."

Eva set her fork down on the table beside her plate and leaned back. Calmly, she looked up at me, but I couldn't read the expression on her face.

"Did you get her pregnant?" she asked quietly.

"I have no fucking idea. I used a condom, so I am leaning toward no. But stranger shit has happened."

"What are you going to do if the baby is yours?"

"I haven't really thought about that. I guess I just feel so confident that it isn't mine that I haven't jumped down that rabbit hole. Garrett is looking into options for requesting a paternity test, but we're also waiting on a few other things first. As of now, the lawsuit is only seeking payment for sexual harassment and for being terminated due to it. It doesn't mention anything about requesting child support, but that doesn't mean that she won't try that route."

"I'm sorry that I didn't allow you to tell me your side of what happened. I freaked out, and I shouldn't have."

"You don't need to apologize. I probably would have reacted the same way, especially given everything you have going on with your sister. I would have told you about it, but honestly, I was hoping it would just be resolved, and I wouldn't have to deal with her again. I've also been instructed not to speak about it, which made it even more complicated."

"I have to admit," she said softly, "I don't know how to take all of this. I mean, what you and I are doing really isn't that different than what you guys were doing."

Her face fell as she turned to look away.

"Eva, what you and I are doing is nothing like what happened with Cora. She was a quick stress reliever—as terrible as that sounds. But she knew what she was doing when she initiated it and confirmed that she only wanted a one-time thing. With you, things are completely different."

"How so?"

"Because with you, I know that I should stay away and leave you alone, but I can't. There's this physical attraction that is so intense that my body knows when you're close by. You're incredibly smart and sexy, and you're possibly the only person I know who can burn toast, but I find all of that so mesmerizing. I'm not the kind of guy who has ever done the whole *committed relationship* thing, but yet I find myself wanting that with you." I blew out a heavy sigh. "And now, because of this fucking lawsuit, I can't do anything about it. I can't be with the one person who I want to be with, even if it's just baby steps toward a relationship."

A beautiful smile pulled across her face as she leaned forward and reached across the table to hold my hand.

"You surprise me, Ethan. But I want to be with you too. Even if you judge my culinary abilities."

She laughed, and I felt the tension start to ease from my shoulders.

"I understand that this lawsuit puts a hindrance on what we've been doing. Do you think it would help if we talked to Regina and let her know what's going on? Then we wouldn't have to hide it or worry about anyone finding out." I could see the hope in her eyes, and I didn't want to be the one who killed it.

"Unfortunately, I think it would only make it worse if we told anyone. I'm being sued by a former employee who claims that I sexually harassed her. I don't think it's going to look good if, not even six months later, I'm dating another employee. It could cost me my reputation, and I just can't risk that."

"I get it," she said, slowly pulling her hand away from mine.

Fuck. This wasn't how I wanted this to go.

"I'm not trying to hurt you," I blew out.

I knew that coming clean and talking things through with Eva would be complicated. Not because she was hard to talk to but because I had somehow created this ridiculous mess that she was now being dragged into. Even if we didn't tell anyone about us, it wasn't fair to her to ask her to be in a relationship with me that we had to keep hidden.

"Please, Eva," I begged, trying to get the hurt look off of her face.

"I think you've said everything you needed to say. Thank you for breakfast." She pushed her food away and stood up, not bothering to look at me as she grabbed her things and walked away.

Twenty-Two
Eva

The day had been long and exhausting as I replayed my conversation with Ethan this morning over and over in my head. It felt like the past few days had been a whirlwind of emotions, from finding out about Cora to Ethan confessing that he wanted a relationship with me. I knew it was immature to walk away at breakfast this morning, but the thought that he wanted to keep me—us—a secret really got to me. I couldn't put my finger on why it bothered me so much because it wasn't like he was trying to hide me for no reason. From a legal standpoint, I clearly understood why he didn't want to tell anyone about our relationship, given the nature of the current lawsuit against him.

Maybe it was that I hadn't really had time to process his confession, or maybe it was that I was still trying to figure out my own feelings about all of it. I wasn't lying when I told Ethan that I wanted to be with him, too, but I never stopped to think about what kind of implication that could have on my career. Starting at a new law firm and sleeping with your boss didn't exactly scream *professional,* and the last thing I wanted was for anyone to question how I got the position I did.

It was almost five o'clock, and Ethan was still in his meeting with Brent and some woman he had brought with him. I assumed it was his girlfriend the way his eyes constantly wandered back to her when she would laugh or smile. My heart ached with the way he looked at her and how his love for her was on display for everyone to see. I couldn't remember the last time anyone had looked at me like that. Perhaps it was never, and at this rate, it didn't seem like that would change any time soon.

I pulled my attention away from the meeting when my phone vibrated on my desk. I looked down to find a text message from Brittany. It was Thursday, which meant she wanted to get together for tacos and margaritas like we did every week. I wrinkled my nose at the thought and swiped my phone to unlock it, hoping that maybe she was sending a text to cancel instead.

Brittany: Tacos and margaritas tonight. I'll meet you at your office in ten minutes.

I groaned and let my head fall back dramatically. It was too late to cancel now if she was meeting me in ten minutes. I sent a quick text back to her confirming that I would see her soon and tossed my phone back on my desk.

My phone vibrated again, and I felt a smidgen of excitement that she had changed her mind after all. Instead, it was a text from Lucy.

Lucy: I talked with Art, and I have a meeting with him on Monday. He spoke with Lance's attorney, and they agreed to start with mediation to see if we can resolve this outside of court first.

Me: Jeremy. He spoke with Jeremy.

I watched for a few minutes as the dots bounced in the text message and then disappeared. Finally, her text came through.

Lucy: Sorry. I know how much you hate talking about him.

Me: I hate even more that he is representing Lance.

Lucy: Me too.

Me: When are you guys doing the mediation?

Lucy: Tuesday at 1:00 in Jeremy's office.

Me: Seriously? Did he push to have it at his office?

Lucy: I didn't ask how they came to an agreement. I'm just going where I'm told to go and praying that Art is as good as your boyfriend says that he is.

Me: He's not my boyfriend.

Lucy: I'm not going to call him the other word. Gabi and Brit can keep that for themselves.

I raised my eyebrows, wondering what they were calling him behind my back.

Me: What do they call him?

The screen started bouncing with dots again, my foot tapping impatiently as I waited.

Lucy: Your f*&@ buddy. That's the best I can do.

I rolled my eyes and let out a chuckle. Movement across the hall caught my eye and I found Brent getting up to shake Ethan's hand as they all said their goodbyes.

"Hey, are you almost ready to go?" Brittany said as she popped into my office, startling me. Had it already been ten minutes?

"Yeah, just give me a second." I sent a quick message back to Lucy, letting her know that I had to go, but we would talk this weekend. I turned off my computer and pulled my purse from the bottom drawer before getting up and walking over to Brittany, who was staring—no, gawking, at Ethan.

"Is that *him*?" she whispered, her eyes wide as if she had just seen a million dollars.

"Yes," I snapped, gently pushing her into the hallway as I pulled my door shut behind me. If we hurried, we could get out of there before Ethan walked out with Brent and the woman he was with.

"You dirty little liar," she hissed, refusing to move as I tried to nudge her down the hallway.

"What did I lie about?" I asked with a high level of annoyance in my tone.

"You said he was attractive, but you failed to mention that he was panty-dropping gorgeous," she scolded, still looking past me. "I can't say that I blame you. I would jump on that every opportunity I had as well."

"Okay, now *you're* being ridiculous. Let's go before they come out, or I'm not taking you for tacos," I warned. I knew that was the keyword to get her ass moving.

"Fine." She sighed heavily and turned to walk with me right as Ethan's door opened and voices carried out.

Shit. We were so close to being able to get out before they saw us.

"Eva, it's nice to see you again," Brent said, stopping me in my tracks.

I closed my eyes and took a deep breath before I turned around to look at him. I shot a quick warning glare at Brittany for her to be on her best behavior as I plastered on the professional smile I had mastered in my first year of law school.

"Brent, it's nice to see you as well. How are you?"

"I'm well, thank you. This is my girlfriend, Chasity." He wrapped a protective arm around her waist as she looked up and gave him a quick smile.

"You must be Eva," she said before giving Ethan a smug smile. "I've heard so much about you."

"It's a pleasure to meet you," I replied as we shook hands.

I looked up at Ethan, wondering what she meant and just *how* much she had heard about me. Ethan scrubbed a hand down the side of his neck as if attempting to wipe away the blush that was creeping up it.

"Well, we were just on our way out," I said politely, smiling as I looked between the three of them. "Have a wonderful evening."

I turned to walk away, thankful for the opportunity to get the hell out of there, when I felt a hand grab my arm and stop me.

"Sorry," Chasity apologized. "I won't keep you. However, Brent and I are having dinner tomorrow night at Zenkichi in Brooklyn and would love it if you and Ethan could join us."

I looked past her over to Ethan and Brent, who both lowered their heads and avoided looking at me. What in the hell happened in that meeting, and why was this woman, who didn't even know me, asking me to have dinner? I could feel the anxiety starting to build as I desperately tried to think of an excuse when suddenly, I was thankful that, for once, I had real plans.

"I'm so sorry. Unfortunately, I can't make it. I have plans with my sisters for dinner and drinks tomorrow night." I pulled my lips together in a sympathetic smile and slightly tilted my head to the side. I watched as Chasity's face fell with disappointment. She glanced over her shoulder before turning back to me.

"Well, maybe another time," she offered as she held her hands together in front of her.

I didn't want to hurt her feelings, and she seemed to be a very sweet person. But not knowing *what* was said about me in that meeting, I had my walls up.

I nodded and was about to turn around to leave when Brittany decided to speak up.

"I actually just got a text message from Gabi that they have to cancel tomorrow night. Jackson is sick." Her voice cracked at the end, and I could hear the lies as she spit them out. I narrowed my eyes at her as I clenched my jaw. She smirked before she continued, "I also have to cancel for tonight. I just found out that my grandmother is visiting from out of town."

I shook my head and then arched an eyebrow at her. She was unbelievable.

"Your grandma is dead," I bit out quietly, but the chuckle from Brent confirmed it was loud enough for everyone to hear.

"Well, we're very spiritual, and we never say no to random visits. So, yeah, I gotta go." She laughed nervously as my icy stare penetrated her soul. Or at least I hoped it did.

She turned on her heel and was down the hallway before I could stop her. I pulled in a calming breath before I turned back to face Chasity. Apparently, there was no way out of dinner with them tomorrow night after all.

"Well, then. I guess I'm free tomorrow night after all." I shrugged my shoulders and tried to smile.

"Actually, since your plans for tonight got canceled as well, did you want to have dinner tonight? Brent and I don't have any plans, and we're already in the city," Chasity said excitedly.

"That's not exactly true," he said with a growl as he reached for her side and tickled her.

"Your plans can wait," she teased with a giggle and shook her head before turning her attention back to me. "Men." She rolled her eyes and sighed, forcing a smile out of me as well. Maybe dinner wouldn't be so bad if I got to spend more time with Chasity and less time with Ethan. The last thing I wanted was for our awkwardness to ruin dinner—especially with a valued client of his.

"So, what do you say, Ethan? Dinner?" Brent asked with a heavy sigh.

"Sure. Why not?" He smiled, but it was the forced one that I had seen him use plenty of times during meetings that he didn't want to be in. He pulled his office door closed behind him as we all walked out to the lobby.

Brent and Chasity walked ahead of us as I pulled back to walk with Ethan. I watched as they held hands and she leaned into him as they waited for the elevator to open.

"What the hell is going on?" I hissed quietly to Ethan.

"I'll tell you about it later," he whispered before he placed his hand on the small of my back and guided me into the elevator.

I tried not to flinch and pull away from his touch, but I also didn't trust myself not to read more into it than there was.

Fifteen minutes later, we were seated in a booth at a quiet, upscale restaurant that I had never been to before. I assumed this was the type of place that required a reservation, yet the woman at the hostess station didn't question Brent as she smiled and led us to our table. My guess was that someone of his caliber didn't require reservations and that they likely had an entire section reserved for when people like him came in. Or maybe that only happened in the steamy billionaire romance books I read.

I shifted in the booth, sliding closer to the wall to put more space between Ethan and me. There was something about being here with him, in the dimly lit room, that felt overly romantic. I wasn't sure if we were here as friends – especially since I didn't know Brent or Chasity at all, or if we were supposed to be here for a business meeting of some sort. I didn't want to risk blurring the lines and letting on that anything had happened between us. Nor did I want Brent to think something was happening between me and Ethan since Ethan was right about needing to uphold his reputation.

After the waitress took our order, I leaned back and tried to relax. It was nerve-wracking not knowing what was going on and why I was there. It felt like everyone else was in on some secret that I had yet to find out about. A few minutes later, our glasses were filled with a wine that likely cost more than the monthly rent of my apartment. My fingers trembled slightly as I reached forward to grab mine at the same time that Ethan reached out to get it for me. I immediately felt the electricity the moment we touched and pulled my hand back. I heard him chuckle as he scooted the glass closer to me and shifted his position so that his leg was touching mine.

I started to pull away when I felt his hand reach down and touch my thigh, forcing me to freeze. What was he doing? Weren't we supposed to be keeping things between us hidden? I looked up at him, my eyes searching his face for an answer. He smiled and winked before looking back at Brent and Chasity. I glanced over and found Brent leaning close to her ear, whispering something that made her giggle as she playfully swatted at him.

"They know about us," Ethan whispered in my ear as he leaned into me. "Chasity was trying to give me advice earlier on how to fix things. I guess she figured it would be best for us to get together and do a double date."

"But we're not dating," I said quietly. "And how do they know about us?"

"Brent and I talked recently. He knew something was off with me. I told him that we were dating but that it was complicated."

I nodded my head, unsure of what to say.

"*Complicated* is an understatement," I said with frustration. Between our conversation this morning and being blindsided by this impromptu dinner, I was more agitated than anything.

"Besides, I thought you didn't want to tell anyone about us?" I raised my eyebrows at him and gave him a pointed look.

"I hadn't planned to tell anyone about us. But for whatever reason, people who know me well seem to be able to figure it out pretty quickly."

He looked across the restaurant and avoided my look before he added, "My mom and Garrett know about us, too."

"What?!" I shrieked rather loudly, the shock of the news hindering my ability to keep quiet. A few people at the tables near us turned to look at what the commotion was before returning to their conversations.

"Everything okay?" Brent asked cautiously, pulling away from Chasity. All eyes were on me now, making me extremely uncomfortable.

"Yes. I'm sorry about that. Ethan was just giving me an update that I hadn't been expecting." I tried to bite back the anger that was trying to force its way out. My face was flushed as I lifted the glass of wine to my lips and took a small sip. The last thing I needed tonight was to get drunk and ruin any future business with Brent for Ethan.

"So, Chasity, what do you do for a living?" I asked, hoping to change the subject and steer the attention away from me.

"I work for Ask Irene. It's an advice column. Have you heard of it?" she asked as she popped a piece of bread into her mouth.

"I've heard of it, but I can't say that I read it often. Sorry," I said with an awkward laugh. My palms were starting to sweat from feeling so stressed out.

"Don't be. I feel like people either read it religiously or have never heard of it. There isn't much of an in-between." She laughed.

"So, am I here for some sort of intervention?" I blurted out, looking between the three of them. "Are Ethan and I here for some expert advice? Or am I missing something?" There was a shrillness in my voice, and I hated how insecure I sounded.

What the fuck was wrong with me? Why did I ask that, and better yet, why wasn't Ethan doing anything to stop me?

"No, nothing like that," she assured me. She took a deep breath and then turned to Brent. "Hey, do you think you can go find the waiter and ask them to bring another bottle of wine?"

"You want me to go track down the waiter to request more wine when you still have a full glass?" He lifted a brow and stared at her with confusion written all over his face.

"Yes. And take Ethan with you, please."

"Because this is a two-man job?"

"Exactly." She gave him a quick nod, which was met with a head shake and a subtle eye roll before he scooted out of the booth. Ethan let out a very loud sigh and followed him.

After they were gone, she lifted her glass of wine and took a sip before turning to look at me.

"Whew, now that they're gone, we can have real girl talk," she said with a little giggle.

"I'm so sorry. I wasn't trying to be rude earlier. Today has been an interesting day, to say the least. It just feels like this week has been a rollercoaster ride that I can't seem to get off of," I explained.

"No worries at all. I can imagine that it's been stressful for you."

I stayed quiet, unsure of what exactly Ethan had told them. The last thing I wanted to do was go blabbering about our personal business and ruin a relationship he had with a client. I nodded and looked away.

"I know that you don't know me and that it probably feels really weird to talk to a complete stranger. I get it. I guess I just felt like I could relate to what you're going through when Ethan was telling Brent what had happened." She paused for a minute and waited for my reaction, but I didn't bother having one. "With Cora—is that her name?"

"Yes. That's her name," I said.

"Brent and I haven't been dating very long, so our relationship is pretty new. And now we're suddenly dealing with his ex and a child that they have together. One that he didn't know about until recently. It's been so hard sorting through everything, and honestly, I've questioned whether I should walk away so he has one less thing to stress over."

"You guys seem so happy together, though," I said quietly.

"We are. I've never been happier. But there's a

child involved, and I could never stand in the way of his relationship with his daughter. I haven't talked to him about any of this, so I would appreciate it if this stayed between us." She blew out a heavy breath. "I don't plan to leave him, so that's not where I was going with this. I just wanted to let you know that I can understand what you might be feeling. Your relationship with Ethan is new and now there's the possibility of him having a child with another woman. That is a hard thing to process. Especially since it can leave you feeling insecure and unsure of what your role is if there's another woman and child in the picture."

I watched as the guys walked through the restaurant, making their way back to the table.

"You're not alone. That's all I wanted to say," she rushed to get the words out before they reached us. "And if you ever need it, feel free to reach out to Ask Irene if you want to talk more." She gave me a quick wink and looked up as Brent slid back into the booth beside her.

"Where's the wine?" she asked, her brows pulled together.

I felt the seat shift next to me as Ethan sat down beside me. He gave me an apologetic smile without saying anything.

"I thought you were just using the wine thing as a hint for us to leave," Brent replied.

"I did." She nodded her head in agreement. "But I also wanted you to get more wine."

I laughed as Brent covered his face with his hands and shook his head. Even though our talk was rushed, I felt better knowing that I wasn't alone in this after all. Here I had sat, studying them and assuming that they were the perfect couple who had everything all figured out, yet they were pretty much just like us. They were uncertain of everything other than their feelings for each other. I looked over at Ethan and met his eyes before reaching down and resting my hand on top of his. He turned his palm over, and for the first time, we held hands without worrying about who might see us.

Twenty-Three
Ethan

"It's a beautiful night," Eva said softly, her hand entwined with mine as I walked her home. Dinner with Brent and Chasity had been unexpected, but by the end of it, none of us were complaining as we said goodbye with genuine smiles on our faces.

"Not as beautiful as you," I replied as I gently squeezed her hand.

She raised an eyebrow and pinned me with a look as we stopped right outside of her apartment building.

"Does that line ever work for you?" she asked, entering her code on the keypad before opening the door.

"It wasn't a line—although I do admit that it sounded corny as fuck. But I meant it. You are very beautiful, Eva."

She smiled at me as she looked over her shoulder and held the door open for me to step inside.

"Do you want to come up for a drink?" she asked with a tiny hint of uncertainty in her voice.

I stalled for a moment as I tried to think rationally about that. It was hard to make a decision when my dick wanted to do all of the talking. But I didn't want Eva to think that all I wanted from her was sex. And if we went back to her place, it was pretty much a guarantee that would be what happened.

"You don't have to," she rushed out as she shifted her purse to her shoulder and tucked a strand of hair behind her ear. "I know it's late, and you've had a long day."

She walked the rest of the way to the elevators and pushed the button as I rushed after her.

"It's not that Eva. I just don't want to overstep."

She pulled her lips into a thin line and nodded as she looked away.

"It's okay. Really. I get it. Thank you for walking me home. I'll see you in the office tomorrow."

The elevator door opened, and she stepped in, lowering her head as she waited for an older couple to exit it. Without thinking it through, I slid inside, barely missing the door as it almost caught me. Her eyes widened in surprise as I stared at her with a hunger I hadn't felt before.

"Eva," I breathed out, almost in warning as I stepped closer to her and wrapped my hand behind her head.

My lips softly pressed against hers as her hands grabbed my shirt and pulled me closer. I took a few steps, pushing her back against the mirrored wall as I continued to devour her mouth. The kiss was intense as our tongues collided, and our hands desperately roamed across each other's bodies. I reached down and grabbed her ass, feeling her mouth turn upward into a smile as I kissed her.

She whimpered as I nibbled her lower lip, my cock straining against my pants as I pressed closer to her so she could feel what she did to me.

"What floor is your apartment on again?" I growled

as I kissed the side of her neck while my hands caressed her breasts, loving the feel of her pebbled nipples through the thin fabric of her shirt. I was impatient to get her naked and on the bed while I did endless things to bring her pleasure.

"Seventeen," she panted, palming my cock and making it harder.

"There's a lot I can do in seventeen floors," I promised.

"Okay," she moaned when my hand slid down and cupped her. "But…"

"But what, baby? Tell me what you want." My breathing was heavy as I lowered my hand and pushed up her skirt, loving how fucking wet she was already. I pushed her panties to the side and ran a finger along her slit, grinning when she hissed.

"The button," she groaned as my finger pushed inside of her.

"Don't worry. I'll work that button for you," I growled heavier this time. Her fingers dug into my shirt as she rotated her hips against my hand.

"No," she panted. "You have to press the button. On the elevator."

I stopped what I was doing and looked at her. Her eyes were dark and hooded, a sexy smile on her face.

"Fuck." I sighed and reached behind me to press the button to her floor. "Don't worry, I'm still gonna press that other button when we get to your apartment."

She laughed and the sweet sound of it filled the elevator. Just as I was about to return to what I had been doing, the elevator stopped on another floor, and the doors opened to allow an older man to get on. I could feel my irritation seeping through me as I glared at him for interrupting us.

"Sorry. This thing takes forever, so I get on whenever I can."

"I agree, it does take forever," Eva replied with a smile as she stood next to me, acting like I hadn't just been fingering her sweet pussy ten seconds before.

What felt like a million years later, the elevator finally made it to her floor. We got out, and she was overly polite, wishing the old man a wonderful night and promising to say hi the next time she saw him. My balls were bluer than a Smurf and ready to burst if she didn't hurry her fine ass up and get inside.

"What do you want to drink?" she asked over her shoulder as she opened the fridge and pulled out a bottle of water.

"You," I said, coming up behind her and wrapping my arms around her waist. I couldn't care less about food or water at this point. Eva was what I needed right now, and I was determined to show her that.

Her body felt more tense when I touched her than it did a few minutes ago in the elevator. It was as if something had changed the second we were alone, and I hated that I didn't have a clue what it was.

"What's wrong?" I asked, letting her go and stepping back to give her space. She turned around and clutched the water bottle to her chest, pursing her lips as she thought about what to say.

"Nothing." She sighed and shook her head.

"Eva, talk to me. Please."

"I enjoy our time together, Ethan, I really do. But do you think that maybe we're getting a little too old for *just sex*?"

I took a few more steps back and leaned against the counter.

"I don't think that we're too old for just sex," I said, watching as her face fell in disappointment. She looked away and refused to meet my eyes. "But Eva, do you really think that this is *just sex* between us?"

"Isn't it? It's not like we go on dates or call each other boyfriend or girlfriend. And on top of that, we have to keep *whatever* this is a secret from everyone. You can't tell me that you think this is anything more than sex."

I nodded my head in agreement and pushed off the counter, taking a few steps toward her until she was pinned against the fridge. This was the conversation that we needed to have, even if I had been dreading it. It wasn't that I didn't want to talk to Eva about all of this. It was that I didn't know how. I'd never been in a serious relationship like this, so it was all new territory for me. The likelihood that I would fuck it all up was pretty high.

"Do you know what I think it is? I think it's me coming to take care of you when you're sick and figuring out how to work remotely from your apartment because I can't stand the thought of something happening to you. It's me pulling strings to get your sister the best family lawyer in Manhattan because I want to help you and support your family. It's having a breakfast date together because you burnt your toast. *Again.* It's lunch dates so that we don't have to eat alone in our offices because I like your company. It's me confiding in you about my fucked-up childhood and telling you the story behind the last gift that my grandma gave me. It's feeling like a complete pussy and talking about my feelings with a client because he's the closest thing I have to a real friend." I took a deep breath and slowly let it out, watching as her eyes reflected the same deep emotion I felt. "So no, Eva. I don't think we're just fucking. I think I'm fucking in love with you, and I have no idea what that even means."

Her eyes softened as she tilted her head to the side and lifted her hand to my cheek.

"I love you too, Ethan. And to be honest, that scares the shit out of me as much as it scares you."

"So, should we just go back to being friends that fuck?" I teased playfully, resting my hand on top of hers.

"Fucking friends might get a little complicated with the whole *love* thing. Besides, you really know how to push my buttons, which probably means that we're already in a relationship." She narrowed her eyes at me.

"Oh baby, trust me. I'm just getting started with the button pushing," I whispered as I leaned close to her ear and nipped it.

"Actions speak louder than words," she countered, acting as if she wasn't at all fazed by my erection pressing against her.

I reached down and grabbed her ass, tossing her over my shoulder as I carried her down the hallway into her bedroom. I playfully tossed her onto the bed, undoing my tie as she laid back on her elbows and watched me. She licked her lips as she watched my fingers work. My eyes traveled down her legs, remembering the feel of her wet pussy under her short skirt in the elevator.

"Open your legs," I instructed, pulling the tie from around my neck.

She pulled her lower lip in between her teeth as she kept eye contact and slowly spread them. Her knees fell to the side, showing me a black lace thong that barely covered her waxed pussy. It was hard not to come right then and there with an image of pure perfection waiting for me on the bed.

I started unbuttoning my shirt slowly as I moved closer to the bed.

"Touch yourself," I said firmly.

"Isn't that your job?" she teased as she pushed her panties to the side and lazily dragged a finger along her slit.

"My job is to make you come harder than you've ever come before. And I won't stop until we have perfection."

"I don't know. No one, and I mean *no one,* can beat Fred."

My eyebrows shot up my forehead as I tried to rein in the jealousy that immediately coursed through me. It wasn't like I expected Eva to be untouched, but I couldn't stand the thought of another man touching her.

"Who the fuck is Fred, and where does he live?"

"Fred is my best friend. Hands down the best lover I've ever had." She continued chewing her lip as her cheeks split into a grin.

"You didn't answer the part about where he lives."

Her fingers continued to stroke her pussy as if she had no worries in the world. All the while, my head felt like it was going to explode as jealousy continued to eat at me.

"He lives in that drawer," she answered, nodding to the nightstand.

I reached over and opened it, glancing at her with a raised eyebrow as I found a handful of vibrators and sex toys.

"Which one is Fred?"

"He's the one that *sucks.* The purple one."

I picked it up and turned it in my hand as I studied it. It was stupid to be jealous of a toy, but knowing that she said it was the best she'd ever had made me immediately want to change that for her.

"What else does it do?" My words felt tight in my throat as I realized how dry it suddenly was.

She pulled her hand away from her pussy and propped herself up on her elbows.

"The long part goes inside of me and stimulates my G-spot."

"Does it make you squirt?" I asked, still flipping it over in my hand to examine all sides of it.

"On occasion. It's kinda hard to hold it in the position I need, so I usually just use the part that sucks."

I pressed the button to turn it on and felt my cock harden as I pressed my finger against it and felt the intense sucking action.

"Fuck," I groaned, tossing my head back.

"What's wrong? Jealous of a toy?"

"Yes," I admitted as I turned it off and set it on the bed. "But I'm about to fix that."

I kept my eyes on her as I finished undressing and climbed up the bed until my face was hovering over her pussy.

"Tell Fred he's being replaced."

She opened her mouth to say something but stopped when I bent down and slid my tongue along her slit. She was already so fucking wet for me that I knew it wouldn't take much to make her come. The problem was that I wanted to spend hours down there, making her come harder than that fucking toy ever had.

I lifted my head and began sucking her clit as I slipped two fingers inside of her. I was no stranger to finding a G-spot, so I immediately began applying pressure where I knew she needed it.

"Fuck," she cried out, her body arching against my touch. "Ethan!"

I sucked harder as her fingers grabbed my hair and pulled while she fought off coming. I knew she was there; I just needed her to let go. I pulled my mouth away slightly as I kept my focus on her G-spot. There was plenty of time to get her off multiple times, but right now, I wanted her to squirt for me.

"Let go, baby," I urged, kissing the inside of her thigh as she tried to close them on me. "Give me that orgasm. Come on my fingers and show me how good you squirt."

"It's too much," she panted, her back lifting higher off the bed.

I changed my position slightly as I kept my fingers where she needed them and used my other hand to press down on her lower stomach.

"Ahhhhh," she moaned loudly. "Shit. This feels too good."

"Relax your body and come, Eva."

"I can't. I can't, Ethan. It's too much."

"It's not too much. You can do this. Relax your mind and your body. Just focus on how good it feels. How good it's going to feel when you come."

I could hear her heavy breathing and knew she was going to need a little more to send her over the edge.

I made sure my hands stayed where they were and kept applying the pressure I knew she needed as I wrapped my lips around her clit and sucked. It wasn't soft and gentle like I typically would have eaten her out. It was hard and demanding, taking her right where I wanted.

She cried out as her body trembled beneath me, and a rush of fluid soaked my face.

Twenty-Four
Eva

I waited until Ethan was comfortable on the bed before I climbed over and straddled him, lifting my skirt in the process. My thong was still pulled to the side, and the way his eyes focused on it told me he liked that I was still wearing it. I reached down and wrapped my hand around his cock, stroking him a few times as he closed his eyes and let out a soft hiss.

I wanted to take my time and enjoy sex with Ethan, but I was too wound up for any *lovemaking* tonight. Right now, I wanted it hard and fast, just like every other time we'd had sex.

I lifted myself, making sure I was lined up before slowly sliding down on his hard cock.

His fingers dug into my hips as he held me steady while I worked on taking my shirt and bra off and tossing them to the floor. My nipples hardened in the cold air, begging for him to suck them.

"I'm not wearing a condom," Ethan said softly, his eyes fluttering open to look at me.

"I know. I'm on birth control and recently had a physical. Nothing to report on my end."

"Same for me. Mine was right after everything happened, and I haven't been with anyone since."

He didn't have to say Cora's name for me to know who and what he was talking about.

I leaned down and kissed him as I began grinding my hips and taking him deeper inside of me. His hands slowly roamed over my ass before one gave it a hard slap, startling me in the best way as heat spread through my core.

I pulled back, leaving my breasts hanging freely in his face as I lined my clit up to rub against his cock. It was the perfect position, and I loved being in control as the friction spread tingles along my spine. He leaned in and eagerly pulled a nipple into his mouth, sucking hard enough to bring me a hint of pain right before I came on his dick.

"Fuck," I whimpered, letting my head fall back as I rode out the waves of pleasure while he took his time torturing my other nipple.

My body was on fire in the best way. Moments later, I felt the warmth spread through me as he gripped my hips and held me in place as he released his load inside of me.

I was, by nature, a planner. Yet everything that happened tonight was totally unplanned, from our dinner double date to him staying the night with me after having several rounds of mind-blowing sex. My body was the most relaxed it had ever been, and I felt calm and at ease having Ethan with me. It felt like we had crossed a lot of hurdles in the past few days, and I was looking forward to where things could go for us. I knew there were still a lot of obstacles ahead of us, including things with Cora, but at least now we both knew how we felt about each other. For now, that was good enough for me.

We sat on the couch watching TV as his fingers lazily stroked my leg, which was resting in his lap. I was tired, but I wasn't willing to call it a night early, not when I had unrestrained access to Ethan. But that also didn't stop the thoughts that kept weighing on my mind now that I had time to sit and think about everything.

"Can I ask you something?" I said, tilting my head up to look at him.

"Of course." His smile was warm and genuine, sending butterflies fluttering through my stomach.

"I know that it's none of my business, but my curiosity keeps getting the better of me." I took a deep breath and blew it out as I sat up straight and looked him in the eye. "What did you talk about with Brent? I mean, as far as *us*."

I expected to feel his body tense beneath me, but instead, he stayed relaxed and trailed a finger up and down my arm as he spoke.

"I don't remember word for word what I said, but I'm pretty sure I was a blabbering idiot. I think that's why Chasity took pity on me and wanted to help. I didn't go into much detail and just kept it simple. I confessed that I was falling in love with you and that things were getting muddled because of another woman. I also didn't go into detail on what was happening with Cora, just that we had a one-night stand, and now she was claiming to be pregnant with my child."

I felt his chest rise and fall behind me as he took a deep breath.

"But I am sorry for discussing what was happening between us with someone else. I didn't mean to disrespect you. I hadn't realized what a complete mess I was until Brent called me out on it and told me that I needed to get my head straight. He was right, obviously. But still, I'm sorry that I didn't know how to talk to you about everything. I haven't been in love like this before, and it scared me."

"I'm glad that it helped you to talk things out with him," I said, feeling somewhat relieved that he had found some comfort in talking to someone that he trusted. In reality, it wasn't much different than me confiding in Brittany, Lucy, or Gabi. They knew everything that happened in my life, and I would probably go crazy if I had to deal with stuff on my own.

"He was easy to talk to, and he didn't judge any of it. Maybe it's because he and Chasity have their own situation going on with his ex, Karly—I don't know. But it felt nice to know that he could relate, and so could she. I knew that she wanted to talk to you; I just had no idea what it was about. For all I knew, she was going to pull you aside and tell you to run for the hills before you got caught up in all of my bullshit."

I laughed and shook my head.

"She didn't say that." I rolled my eyes as I looked up at him. "She just reminded me that relationships aren't perfect, and if you want to be with someone, you have to make it work. It takes both people to put in the effort, though."

It reminded me of my relationship with Jeremy and how no matter how hard I tried to fix us, we couldn't be fixed because he didn't care. He never put in the effort and I didn't see that until now.

"I'm willing to put in the work," he said, freeing me from my thoughts.

"Me too." I smiled and squeezed his hand, which was still resting on my leg.

"Hey, have you heard anything from your sister about Art? Has she reached out to him yet?" he asked, changing the subject for me.

"Yeah," I said, clearing my throat. "She has a meeting

with him on Monday, and then they're meeting at Jeremy's office on Tuesday to start mediation. I forgot to ask if it would be okay if I took a longer lunch that day to go with her?"

He let out a heavy sigh and squeezed my hand.

"I don't think that's a good idea."

I pulled my head back and tilted it to the side to look at him.

"Why not? If it's about the time I'm missing in the office, I'll stay late to make up the hours."

His face softened as he looked at me.

"Eva, it's your ex-fiancé and your sister. There's no way that you can attend the meeting without letting your personal feelings get in the way. That could completely jeopardize things for your sister. Art is an amazing attorney—the best of the best. But he can't do his job if you create additional complications that he can't fix. The last thing you want is for your ex to go after your sister in retaliation."

I closed my eyes and leaned my head back against the couch. He was right. I didn't know why I hadn't thought of it.

"I didn't think about it that way," I admitted. "But she's my baby sister, and she needs help. How can I not help her? I have to protect her."

"You are helping her by staying out of it. She has the best lawyer in Manhattan. Let him do his job."

"How am I supposed to just step back and walk away from this?" I asked, not expecting an actual answer to my rhetorical question.

"You're not. You just have to be there for her in

a different way," he said softly. "Instead of going to the mediation with her, maybe you can take her to dinner when it's over? You can still be there for her and support her. Just not in the same room as your ex or her husband. Don't give them any more ammunition than they already have."

"I know," I said and sighed.

"It's hard, I get it. I really do. But she will get through this. I promise."

"If anything were to happen to her or Jackson…"

"It won't," he interrupted. "You just have to have faith and allow the system to do what it's supposed to do."

"I guess you're right. It seems like there's a lot of trust that we're having to put into the system these days."

I felt his body stiffen next to me and knew that I had hit a chord. I wasn't trying to, but his situation with Cora wasn't over, either. It also required us to trust the system and have faith that everything would work out as it was supposed to. Little did we know that our faith was about to be severely tested in the blink of an eye.

Twenty-Five
Ethan

I spent the first half of Friday morning on the phone with Brent as we worked out the last few details of the Watson Investments deal. I was more than somewhat relieved when he let us off the hook for dinner at Zenkichi tonight. Not that I didn't want to spend time with him and get to know Chasity. I just wanted to spend that time alone with Eva. I had no idea if she really had plans with her sisters or whether they had been canceled. Either way, I was determined to find out.

My fingers tapped against the keyboard in front of me as I struggled to think about how to ask her. Everything sounded lame and pathetic in my head. I was a fucking lawyer who had graduated at the top of my class, yet I couldn't figure out how to ask the girl I loved if she had plans tonight.

I moved the mouse around until a new chat box was opened on my desktop.

Me: Hey, what's happening tonight?

I stared at the words on the screen and rolled my eyes. What was I? Seventeen? I pressed the arrow to delete the string of text and then tried again.

Me: Any big plans for the night?

Yeah, like that was any better. Another long press of the arrow to get rid of the pitiful words in front of me.

Me: Hey

Without realizing it, I hit the enter key with my wrist and sent the message. I lowered my head and felt the heat of her gaze as I looked up and found her looking into my office from her desk.

Eva: Hey

Well, at least this was a start—an awkward one, but one nonetheless.

Me: Sorry, I accidentally hit send before I finished typing.

Eva: No worries. Did you need something?

Yeah, a fucking brain CT or scan or whatever they do to see if you're crazy. I had felt off all day and couldn't figure out why. Last night with Eva had been incredible. Yet I still couldn't shake the feeling that something was amiss.

Me: No, thank you.

She turned to look at me with a puzzled look on her face after she read the message.

Don't worry, Eva, I'm as fucked up right now as I sound.

I blamed her wet pussy that had been wrapped around my cock so many times last night, it must've somehow sucked all of my intelligence out with each orgasm she pulled from me.

I put my head down between my hands and tried to figure out what I was doing. Maybe I needed carbs? I had skipped breakfast this morning in an effort to run by my place to shower and change clothes, which made me later than I wanted to be.

"Hey, are you alright?" she asked softly as she leaned against the door frame.

I lifted my head and looked at her. She stood there looking fucking gorgeous with her long, black hair in loose curls that laid perfectly over the crimson red sleeveless blouse she was wearing. It was tucked into a tight black skirt that showed off the curves I had taken my time tracing with my tongue last night.

I swallowed hard, trying to use whatever mental power I had left to force my dick down. Now wasn't the time or place for this. I had a lot I needed to get done, and fucking her in my office wasn't on my list. Even though it should have been.

"Yeah, I'm sorry. I'm just a little out of sorts this morning," I mumbled and ran a hand over the coarse hair on my jaw. Was it still morning? Who even knew what time it was at this point?

"Did you eat breakfast?" Her brows pulled together in concern. "I can make you some—"

"Please don't say toast." I scrunched my face and laughed.

She pretended to be hurt as she pouted and folded her arms over her perfect tits, pinning me with a look.

"Fine. I can order breakfast from somewhere. What do you want?"

"You don't have to order food for me. Besides, isn't that Kate's job?"

"Kate is in Regina's office. She's been there all morning." She leaned back slightly and looked down the hall to make sure she wasn't at her desk. "I don't know when she'll be back."

"What's that about?" I asked out loud, even though I hadn't expected her to know.

"I have no idea. Kate seemed a little off this morning. Kind of distant with me. Who knows?" She shrugged and scrunched her nose. "So, what do you want for breakfast? Or would you rather wait, and I'll order us lunch?"

I glanced down at the clock on my computer and was surprised to find that it was already almost eleven.

"Why don't we just do lunch since it's already almost that time?"

"Sounds good. Let me know what you want, and I'll put in an order." She smiled and turned to walk back to her office. I felt the temperature in the room rise about one hundred degrees when I caught a glimpse of her ass in the tight skirt with the little slit at the bottom. She was killing me with this outfit and didn't even know it.

"Eva," I croaked out, coughing to try to clear my throat.

"Yeah?" She turned around and stepped back to where she was standing a few seconds ago.

"You look really nice today," I blurted out. "I like that outfit."

My eyes wandered her body and I enjoyed the look on her face as she recognized what I was really trying to say.

"Thank you," she said quietly, walking over to my desk.

She was inches away from me, the scent of her vanilla body wash floating in the air around me.

"I was worried that this skirt might be inappropriate for the office."

She walked behind my desk and sat on the edge as I turned in my chair to look at her. Her legs were in between mine, and I could easily see up her skirt without anyone having any idea what I was doing.

"Why would it be inappropriate?" I asked, my voice low and gruff.

She glanced over her shoulder before looking back at me, a devious smile on her face. Slowly, she planted her feet further apart, her heels digging into the carpet below her. I looked down and fought the urge to run my hand up her smooth, tanned legs as she spread them a little further for me. I could almost see whether or not she was wearing panties, but she wasn't sitting back far enough, and she knew it.

"I was worried that it might be too… short. And tight." She sighed dramatically and flipped her hair over her shoulder before she tilted her head and slowly turned her body toward me. "It was hard finding the right panties to wear because, us girls, we really hate panty lines."

"What panties did you decide on?" My breathing grew heavy as I reached up to pull at my tie, which suddenly felt way too tight.

"None." She leaned back further and spread her legs wide for me, showing me her bare pussy.

"Fuck, Eva," I growled as I scooted closer and ran my hand up her thigh. I could see the desire in her eyes, the same need coursing through her that was pulsing through my veins right now.

"I know what I want for lunch," I said quietly, watching her face as I slipped a finger inside of her.

She gasped at the contact before she rolled her head back and let it fall. I slid another finger in, my dick twitching in response to the way her pussy grabbed hold of my fingers the same way it did with my cock last night. She moaned quietly as I fucked her with them for a few minutes, driving her as wild as she was driving me.

I slowly pulled them out and held them up to her face, showing her how wet they were.

"Taste yourself, Eva," I demanded. "See how good you taste."

She hesitantly opened her mouth before slowly taking my finger inside and sucking it. The action went straight to my cock as she twirled her tongue around and sucked harder. Unable to take it anymore, I pulled my hand back and scooted my chair closer to her.

"The door is open, so you're gonna have to be really quiet," I said sternly, looking at the excitement on her face before I lowered my head in between her legs. She let out a moan as she ran her fingers through the back of my hair.

"Quiet," I warned. "Or someone will catch us."

I knew how much it had turned her on when we fucked in front of the window, so it didn't surprise me that she wouldn't be drenched with the thought of someone walking in and catching me as I ate her out on my desk.

Slowly, I ran my tongue along her folds, licking up and down each side before parting her with my fingers and sliding them inside. I felt her hips buck in response and let out a low chuckle. While I worked my fingers against her G-spot, I focused my tongue on her clit as I rotated between gentle licks and hard sucking. I knew her body well enough now to know what she needed to get her to a quick climax.

Her hips rotated around my face as she tried to get as much friction as possible the closer she got. I fucked her faster with my fingers as I went straight to sucking her clit. Within seconds I could feel her pussy spasm around me as she came undone on my desk. I pulled back and wiped my face with the back of my hand, feeling good about the satisfied look on her face. She sat upright and closed her legs as she giggled.

I was riding the high of it when I heard footsteps coming down the hallway and knew that we didn't have time to get her out of my office before whoever it was got here. Thankfully, Eva heard them at the same moment I did and jumped off the desk, standing beside me as I scooted my chair back to face my computer.

"See, right there. That's what I was talking about," Eva said as she pointed to the Eiffel Tower on my wallpaper. I quickly moved the mouse and clicked open a report I had been working on earlier to make it look more believable as Regina stepped into my office.

Eva stood upright and smiled at Regina as if she hadn't just committed one of the most inappropriate office activities in the handbook.

"Thanks, I was trying to find that in the report but must have skimmed right over it," I said to Eva, loud enough for Regina to hear. I turned my full attention to Regina and attempted to smile.

"Hello, Regina. What can I do for you?" I asked cautiously. She looked between us, a look of concern on her face mixed in with the stoic expression I was used to seeing from her when we were meeting with an employee that we had to let go. The last time I saw that look was when we met with Cora.

"I need to speak with you—both of you, in my office." She turned on her heel and walked out, leaving us in stunned silence.

"Do you think she knows what just happened?" Eva

whispered with panic laced in her voice.

"No. It must be something else. She wasn't close when you were coming on my face, so she didn't see or hear anything," I said to reassure her, only to get a jab in the ribs with her elbow. "What? You can't say that didn't happen."

"You're impossible," she said and shook her head. At least her mood seemed a little less tense as we made our way to Regina's office.

When we got there, she was already sitting at her desk, looking over the rim of her glasses to read something on her computer. She briefly looked up when she saw us before returning her attention to the computer.

"Come in and close the door," she instructed sharply.

Eva walked in before me and took the seat closest to the wall while I closed the door and took the other seat. Regina's fingers typed quickly before she moved her mouse and turned her attention to us. There was a look of anger and disappointment on her face, which made me question what had happened with Kate and, more importantly, why we were there.

"It has been brought to my attention that the two of you have been engaging in activities that are not permitted at work. With that being said, I've also received a formal complaint about it."

She reached over and picked up a piece of paper, then slid it across the desk to Eva and me. I quickly scanned the document, unable to believe what I was reading.

"You've got to fucking be kidding me," I muttered before looking up at Regina. "Are you serious?"

Eva continued reading, absorbing every word as I had stopped halfway through. I had seen enough.

"No, unfortunately, this is not a joke. Kate has filed a

sexual harassment complaint against you and Eva due to the unprofessional and sexually inappropriate work environment you have created," Regina said, looking down to read her copy in front of her. She set it down, leaned back in her chair, and looked at us.

"Just give it to me straight, you guys. What's going on?" she asked.

I swallowed hard and looked at Eva who looked pale as she stared at Regina. I couldn't believe this was happening, let alone with Kate. She was the only personal assistant who had been with me for over ten years and never once had an issue with me. All this time, I trusted her to do her job and mind her fucking business.

"Look—whatever you guys are doing on your own time, that's none of my business. But this complaint claims that you're doing this on company time, which, unfortunately, makes it my business. I can't help you if I don't know what's going on. So please, let me help you."

I leaned back in the chair and closed my eyes. This was going to turn into another fucking nightmare that I didn't need.

"Eva and I have been dating. Unofficially until last night, I guess?" I said bitterly. I hated talking about my personal business, and I hated even more that, thanks to Kate, Eva was now being forced to discuss hers.

"When did it start?" Regina asked, grabbing her notepad and pen from the end of her desk. Her hand was lifted above the paper while she waited for an answer.

"It's complicated. I don't know that there was an actual start date," I blew out.

"I get that this is hard, and it's very personal. But given what's happening with Cora…" She gave me a look and raised her eyebrows as she refrained from saying anything further in front of Eva.

"She knows about Cora and the sexual harassment lawsuit," I confirmed. "Eva and I first hooked up a few weeks before she started working here. It was a random encounter at a nightclub, and neither of us thought that we would see each other again. We didn't exchange information and had no contact until the day she started working here."

"Okay, what else," Regina said as she wrote the information down. Eva sat quietly in the chair beside me as she chewed on her fingernail.

"We've been trying to keep our relationship professional, especially with everything going on with Cora. Unfortunately, we found it impossible to stay away from each other. This connection is too strong for us to fight it."

"Have you had sex at work?"

Her question was asked so nonchalantly, like asking someone if they wanted ketchup on their burger. Eva looked like she was on fire, given how red her face and neck were from embarrassment.

"Yes," I bit out.

"I'm sorry. I know these questions are hard to answer. Trust me, I don't want to ask them any more than you want to answer them. But with everything else going on, I need all of the facts you can give me. Otherwise, it's going to turn into hearsay, and we don't need that right now. Can you tell me how many times and where?"

"Is that really fucking necessary?" I shouted, slamming my hands down on the desk and startling everyone.

Regina set her pen down and folded her hands on top of the notepad, giving me a few minutes to calm myself down.

"In addition to her complaint, Kate also provided me with copies of this," Regina said calmly as she slid another piece of paper over to me. I pinched my nose and closed my eyes when I saw that it was the dirty chat message between Eva and me.

"How did she get these?" I asked, frustrated.

"I don't know. She wasn't willing to tell me when I asked. But rest assured that I will have our IT department look into this. In the meantime, I strongly suggest that you change your passwords and lock your office when you're not in it."

"Will do." I scrubbed my hand down my face.

"Am I fired?" Eva asked suddenly, looking up at Regina with tears in her eyes.

"No, you're not fired." She shook her head and then sighed. "While this breaks numerous rules in our handbook, the repercussions of firing you for having a relationship with your boss would not be good for the company right now. I will have to speak with the board of directors, and there may be disciplinary action. However, I won't know what that is until I meet with them."

"So, everyone is going to know that we've been sleeping together. At work. Outside of work." Her voice trailed off as she turned to look at the wall.

I reached over to grab her hand before she jerked it away from me. I couldn't blame her for being upset over this. I was just as furious and embarrassed about it, but I never meant for her to have her reputation on the line as a result.

"Can either of you remember any times when you left your office unattended or your computer unlocked? If we can narrow down the window, it will help us to gather all of the facts before this goes any further."

"I think I know exactly when it happened," Eva muttered, turning back to look at Regina.

"Okay," Regina said as she urged her to continue.

"After *that* happened," she replied, nodding to the paper on the desk with our chat. "I went to the bathroom to freshen up. I hadn't bothered to lock my computer or close my door since I was going to be quick. When I got back to my office, Kate was standing next to my printer. She claimed that sometimes the network messed up and that her report was sent to my printer. I didn't think anything about it until now."

I tried to think back to that day and whether or not I had seen Kate in her office, but I was drawing a blank. Perhaps it happened when I had made a quick trip to the bathroom myself.

"Thank you for the information. I will look into this and let you know what we find," Regina said as she wrote the information down.

"Do you need anything else from us or are we good to wrap this up and keep a shred of our dignity intact?" I asked sarcastically, already feeling beyond drained from this meeting.

"I think that's all I need for now. Since we have an idea of when Kate had access to the chat message, I don't see any reason that we need the details of any other situations that may have occurred during office hours. But in the meantime, try to keep your distance from one another while you're on the clock."

We nodded in agreement before standing up to leave. I wanted to grab Eva and take her somewhere private to talk about what had just happened, but that would immediately be going against what Regina just asked us not to do.

"What's going to happen with Kate? Will she still be

our assistant?” Eva asked as she stood by the door without opening it.

“No. Effective immediately, she’s been reassigned to another lawyer in the firm. I will start looking for a replacement as soon as possible.”

“I’m sure I’m not the most reliable or credible person right now, given everything that has happened. But I might know someone interested and can start right away.” She glanced back at me nervously.

“I still think highly of you, Eva,” Regina assured her. “Who is it?”

“My sister, Lucy. She currently works as a receptionist at the hospital. However, she could really use a job with set hours so she could take care of her son, Jackson.”

I felt the vein in my head throb as I listened, wondering what in the hell she was doing. Why hadn’t she talked to me about this before bringing it up to Regina?

“Do you think that you and your sister could work together without letting your personal life get in the way?” I asked her, ignoring the look that I got from Regina.

“I work with *you,* don’t I?” she said curtly before turning and walking away.

Twenty-Six
Eva

My hands were shaking as I made it back to my desk and sat down. I was trying to pick an emotion and stick with it, but it felt impossible when there was a constant battle between anger and humiliation pulsing through me simultaneously. I unlocked my computer and opened my email, trying to force myself to focus and forget about everything that had just happened.

A few seconds later, a chat box popped up and flashed in the lower corner of the screen. I glanced across the hall to see if Ethan was looking at me, but he seemed rather focused on whatever he was reading on his computer. I moved the mouse and clicked on it, relieved to see that it was from Regina and not Ethan.

Regina: When you have a chance, please forward me your sister's contact information. I will reach out to her as soon as possible.

I felt the tension release from my shoulders as I typed my response back to her, thanking her for considering my sister for the position. I knew that Regina would still need to interview other candidates as well and that there was a good chance that they wouldn't pick Lucy for the position, but I still had to try.

Lucy had been working for the hospital for eight years. While they were flexible with her when she first had Jackson, they'd recently started giving her a hard time about her requested shifts. Instead of letting her work during the week, they would assign her the weekend shifts or the graveyard shifts. Both of these would make it impossible for her to work as a single mother. I knew this would be something that Lance would use against her to prove that she wasn't able to provide a stable environment for Jackson. I wasn't about to let that happen if there was anything that I could do about it.

I sent a quick email to Regina with her information and then sent Lucy a text to let her know what was going on. I felt excited that maybe something good would happen for once, and Lucy would get the job. After the bullshit that happened today, I needed something good. I felt bad for not talking to Ethan about bringing Lucy on before I mentioned it to Regina, but in all fairness, it wasn't like there was a position to consider her for until now. There was an opportunity, and I took it.

Was he right that we wouldn't be able to work together without letting our personal lives get in the way? Maybe. Honestly, I didn't know. I was five years older than her, and that seemed to work well for us growing up because we were never into the same things at the same time. But, on the flip side, she had also complained a lot that I was more like a second mother than a sister, so there was that.

The day dragged on, and I was ready for it to be over so that I could go home and drink some wine before sulking in my apartment all weekend. My phone vibrated on the desk, alerting me to a new text message. I picked it up and swiped it open to find a group message between Lucy, Gabi, Brittany, and myself.

Gabi: Are we still meeting for dinner and drinks tonight?

I decided to respond as quickly as I could before anyone could get the bright idea to make this happen tonight. I wasn't in the mood for it and desperately just wanted some alone time.

Me: Brittany told me it was canceled last night. I already made other plans. Sorry.

Brittany: I said that so you would go to dinner with your sexy fuck buddy and his friends. Those better be your plans. If not, dinner with us is still on.

Gabi: Agreed. Go to dinner with your fuck buddy, and let's do brunch in the morning?

I exhaled heavily and pulled my shoulders back. I wasn't in the mood to deal with this.

Me: We had dinner last night instead after Brit ducked out and stood me up. I have other plans tonight. We'll catch up later this weekend. K?

Lucy: What's going on? Why don't you want to meet up with us?

Gabi: Maybe she's tired from all of her friends with benefits action?

Brittany: He is DELICIOUS. I'm just saying I would be tired after a night with him, too. You can bet that I would be buying an ALL-DAY pass for that ride...

Me: Alright, well, you ladies enjoy dinner. I'll talk to you later.

I put my phone down and closed my eyes as I rubbed the back of my neck. Today was turning out to be more of a disaster than I thought. I prayed that they would sense my bitter attitude in the group text message and stop asking to meet up tonight.

My phone continued to vibrate on my desk as they

continued to send messages. I didn't bother to check them as I held out hope that they would just leave me alone.

By five o'clock, I was ready to go home and fall into bed. My stomach growled loudly, reminding me that I had missed lunch. But I was in such a bad mood that I had no desire to do anything about it. I grabbed my purse and turned my computer off, making sure to check the screen to confirm it was really off this time. I felt stupid for being so foolish to have left it unlocked, to begin with. Had I been smarter, all of this might have been avoided, and I wouldn't have to worry about the entire office knowing that I was fucking my boss.

I flipped the light switch to turn off the lights as I stepped into the hallway and pulled the door closed behind me. Ethan's office was already empty, his door closed, and lights turned off. I didn't remember seeing him leave, but I also tried my hardest to avoid him as much as I could today.

As I turned to walk down the hall, I felt a body as I collided against it. My hand flew to my chest as I took a step back.

"Lucy!" I shrieked, my eyes wide with surprise. "What the hell are you doing here?"

"I came down to meet with Regina. We just finished a few minutes ago. I thought I would come see if you were still here and drag you out to dinner if your other plans fell through." She winked as if she knew my secret and locked her arm in mine as she led me down the hall.

"Why didn't you tell me you were coming to meet with her?" I asked, trying to get my heart rate back down. I decided to ignore the last part about going to dinner. If I pretended not to hear her, then she couldn't get mad when I refused to go… right?

"It was so last minute I didn't have time. I got Jackson to Mom's house and rushed right over."

"So, how did it go?" I could feel the hope radiating through me as I reached out and pressed the button for the elevator.

She pulled in a deep breath and waited for the doors to open before she jumped in and turned to face me.

"I got the job!" she squeaked excitedly, doing some awkward cheerleader pose as I laughed and joined her in the elevator. I pressed the button for the lobby before reaching over to hug her.

"That's amazing, Lucy. I'm so happy for you!"

"Thank you for recommending me for the job," she said as her cheeks continued to split with her grin. "Now, I can finally quit the hospital and work a real job with real hours."

The elevator jerked before it stopped, and the doors slid open to the empty lobby. We got off and walked arm in arm to the front of the building, where a security guard was waiting by the door. I smiled and nodded hello as he opened the door and held it for us.

"Thank you. Have a great weekend," I said to him as we left the building and walked down the sidewalk. "You have a real job. It has just recently turned into a sucky one."

"Yeah, but it's been the same thing for years. I started there with little office experience, so it was a great way to learn. But after eight years, I haven't been promoted or moved up. It's time for a change. I can't just stay because I'm comfortable."

"I get it," I replied softly as we walked down the street. "It's hard to want change when you're used to doing things a certain way." I stopped and opened my arms for a hug goodbye so I could go on my way back to my apartment while she went wherever she was going. Either way, I knew she wasn't taking the same train as me.

"What are you doing?" she asked as she folded her arms over her chest and narrowed her eyes at me.

"This is where I leave you." I sighed playfully, raising my brows and opening my arms wider for her to get the not-so-subtle message.

"This is the train you take to your apartment," she said dryly. "Which means that you don't have plans after all."

I waited for a moment and took a deep breath. If I could pull in enough of whatever positive energy I had left in me, maybe I could muster the older sister vibe that usually worked with her.

"I do have plans. I'm taking time for myself tonight. Self-care. I have a date that's long overdue and includes pampering and relaxation."

"I don't think so. You're going to dinner with us. Even if I have to throw you over my shoulder and carry you like a four-year-old having a tantrum," she warned sternly.

"Are you comparing me to your child?" I pulled my head back and eyed her suspiciously.

"You're the one acting like him…" She tapped her foot impatiently on the concrete in front of her.

"Why can't I just go home and enjoy my night by myself? It's been a long week, and I really don't feel like being social," I whined.

When that didn't work, I stuck out my bottom lip and pouted.

"Because Eva, you know as well as I do that you're not going to go home and do anything productive. You're going to attempt to make dinner but then realize that you don't have any groceries. Then you'll try to make toast and catch your apartment on fire. While you're eating your burnt dinner, you'll try to convince yourself that you're going to watch something happy and uplifting. Instead, you'll sit and binge-watch true crime shows while making lists of everyone that might be trying to kill you."

I rolled my eyes and blew out a breath. She was right, and she knew it. The only thing that she had wrong was that I would make toast, and that was only because that was my attempt at dinner last night. The joke was on her because tonight, I had a full menu planned with multiple courses involving Ben and Jerry's.

"I really don't want to go." I quirked a brow and challenged her to a stare-down.

"Yeah, and I really don't want to go home when we're done and fight with Jackson about why he can't take his pet goldfish to bed. We all do things we don't want to Eva. But at least this leads to you having real food and some girl talk to get all of that stress off your shoulders." She stepped closer and reached her hands out to hold mine. "Is it really that bad that your sisters and best friend want to spend time with you and make sure you're okay?"

I rolled my eyes and shook my head. She was good.

"Fine," I said through clenched teeth. "I will go. But I'm having a margarita. Or two."

She laughed and jumped excitedly before looping her arm in mine again as she dragged me down the sidewalk.

"You can have as many as you want. Tonight, we are celebrating new beginnings! And Lord knows I need one."

"Things haven't been that bad for you, have they? I mean, aside from Lance," I said his name warily, a taste of hatred heavy on my tongue.

"No, they haven't been bad, per se. But I realized that by staying complacent, I wasn't living my life. I wasn't happy. With my marriage. With my job. It was time to make changes and live a life that I actually want to live."

"What's that supposed to mean?" I asked, narrowing my eyes at her.

"No, nothing like that," she said dismissively and waved her hand at me. "I'm not talking about being suicidal or anything. I just meant that I've been so unhappy for so long that I didn't even realize I wasn't happy. That's not fair to me or Jackson. He deserves a mom who can teach him how to enjoy life, and I wasn't doing that."

I reached down and squeezed her hand.

"Everything is going to be alright," I assured her.

"I know," she whispered with a smile.

A few train stops later, we were seated in the back of Tia Rosa's Cantina. I tried to keep my frustration under control when I saw Gabi and Brittany already at the table, drinking margaritas and eating chips and salsa.

"There better be chips and salsa left for us," I warned somewhat playfully before I plopped down in the decorative metal chair and hung my purse off the back of it. At that moment, a waiter came by and set a new basket of chips and salsa on the table in front of me. I smiled and looked up to order a margarita when someone caught my eye.

I leaned forward and looked past the waiter, unable to process what I was seeing. I could hear the girls talking around me, but everything sounded muted as the blood rushed through my head. There was no fucking way this was happening. I grabbed my phone and opened the camera, taking as many pictures as I could, praying that at least one of them would be in focus.

Sitting on the other side of the restaurant was Cora, cuddled up in a booth with Kate. They were completely oblivious to me being there as Cora pulled her in closer to her and planted a long kiss on her lips. I switched the camera to video, knowing that this would be concrete evidence to pass along to Regina and our legal team.

After our meeting this morning, I had a gut feeling that there was more to the story than what we had been told. It didn't make sense how or why Kate would randomly end up in my office after what we had done. I had spent the day trying to figure out what had given us away and why she would think of snooping around my office the second I walked out.

"Ma'am?" a man's deep voice interrupted my thoughts. I lowered my phone and looked up to see the waiter standing beside me, impatiently tapping his foot as his hand hovered over the notepad he was using to collect our orders.

"I'm sorry. What?" I croaked; my throat suddenly dry.

"May I have your drink order, ma'am?"

"Oh, yes. I'll have a house margarita. Please."

I felt like a blubbering idiot, unable to focus on anything other than Kate and Cora sitting snuggled up close together across the room. He walked away and my attention went back to getting more video as the girls talked around me as if I wasn't there. Which, to be honest, I wasn't.

I pinched my fingers on the screen of my phone, zooming it in as far as it would go without distorting the image. Kate said something that got Cora laughing, her blonde hair spilling down her back as she tilted her head back to laugh. They were both young, beautiful women, and I was stumped trying to figure out why they would go after Ethan for sexual harassment when obviously neither of them were interested in him. Any onlooker could easily see how obsessed they were with each other as they leaned in for another kiss, not giving a damn about anyone else in the room.

I took a few more pictures, then lowered my phone before someone caught me and turned me in for being a creeper. Part of me wanted to forward the pictures and video immediately to Ethan, but the other part of me was still upset over everything that had happened today. I knew that I didn't have any reason to be mad or upset with him, but that didn't stop me from avoiding him like the plague.

I was embarrassed about getting caught and having to admit that I had broken a handful of rules that could have easily cost me my job. Even though *don't fuck your boss in his office* wasn't explicitly written in the handbook, I'm sure it was assumed that it didn't need to be said. I had officially become one of those people who were responsible for the absurd and ridiculous rules that were added in because common sense was lacking.

"So, what do you think?" Gabi asked, staring at me with such intensity that I was sure she could read my mind at that moment.

"I'm sorry. About what?" I leaned back as the waiter slid my margarita in front of me and walked away. Perfect timing.

"Lucy and your fuck buddy," Gabi said as she sighed. "What do you think of them together?"

I frowned as I took a sip, trying to figure out what the hell she was talking about.

"Stop calling him that. It grosses me out," Lucy complained, smacking Gabi's arm. "I don't want to think about him that way when I start my first day on Monday."

"I wouldn't mind thinking about him that way." Brittany giggled. "He. Is. HOTTT!"

I rolled my eyes playfully and took another drink, allowing the alcohol to crawl through my veins and bring me the numbness that I needed.

"I haven't seen him yet. Or met him." Lucy's eyes widened as she continued. "Oh my God, what if he hates me? What if he fires me on my first day?"

"He's not going to fire you. Calm down." I laughed as I rested my hand on her arm and tried to reassure her while the alcohol played with my head. I looked across the restaurant, keeping an eye on Cora and Kate to make sure they hadn't spotted me. "Just stay focused and do your job. You'll be fine."

"Yeah, and maybe don't sleep with him like your sister did?" Brittany joked, earning a kick under the table from me.

"Ouch!" Gabi yelped and lowered her hand under the table to rub her leg.

"Sorry." I pulled my lips into a tight smile and shrugged. "I was aiming for Brit."

"I'm not going to sleep with him. I'm not that kind of girl, and you know that." Lucy shook her head and frowned.

I felt the heat flush across my face with embarrassment as they all turned to look at me.

"Sorry," she said quickly. "I didn't mean anything by that—"

"It's fine," I said, putting my hand up to stop her. "But if it's all the same, can we please talk about something other than Ethan? ANYTHING other than Ethan."

Brittany changed the subject to her trip to Miami and all of the gorgeously tanned guys that she had met. The waiter came to take our orders, putting a halt to her overly risqué story about the one-night stand she had before she left. I tried to focus and pay attention, but I was still distracted by everything that had happened. When I looked over at Kate and Cora's table, they were gone. With a deep breath, I opened my phone and sent a text message to Ethan, asking if we could talk.

Twenty-Seven
Ethan

I was still waiting for Eva to call after I texted her back to confirm that I was still up. Her text was short and to the point, which made me anxious to be able to talk to her after she spent the day avoiding me. A few minutes later, my phone vibrated on the coffee table before my hand darted out and grabbed it. Without bothering to check the caller ID, I slid the button across the phone to answer it.

"Hello?"

"Hey," she said breathlessly before hiccupping.

"Is everything alright?" I asked, trying to get a feel for where she was at and why she sounded so winded. "Where are you?"

"Yup," she replied, followed by another hiccup. "You're so nosey." She giggled.

I scrubbed my hand down my face as I stood up and paced in front of the couch. She sounded tipsy, if not drunk. Eva didn't just giggle randomly when she was still pissed at me, so I could only guess that alcohol had taken the edge off for her.

"Where are you, Eva?" I asked again.

"I'm walking Lucy home."

"From where?"

"From Tia Rosa's. We had margaritas," she announced proudly. She was definitely buzzed.

"I'm glad it sounds like you've had a good night." I felt myself smiling, genuinely happy that she hadn't had as piss-poor of a night as I had. "Can I send someone to pick you ladies up and make sure you get home safely?"

I didn't want to overstep by offering to come for them myself. It was a step in the right direction that she was willing to talk to me. I didn't want to ruin that by being too pushy.

"No. We are fine. We don't need men shining in their armor to come get us." Hiccup.

I felt the corners of my lips curl up into a smile as I kept from laughing.

"Got it," I said lightly, just thankful to hear her voice. "Was there something you wanted to talk to me about?"

"Yes. And it's important. Like super mind-blowing out of this world important." Hiccup. "Be careful, or you're going to fall." Her voice was quieter as she pushed the phone away from her mouth to talk to someone else.

"Are you sure I can't send someone to come for you guys?" My worry was increasing the longer I talked to her and realized just how buzzed—or drunk—she really was.

"We're fine," she assured me as she laughed. "We just got to my parent's house, and Lucy forgot about the stairs up the porch."

"Since Lucy is home safe, why don't I come get you and take you home?" I offered, desperate to see her.

"I might just stay here. I haven't decided yet." I hated the thought of her trying to get herself home like this. If I knew where her parents lived, I would already be on my way there to take care of her, whether she wanted me to or not.

"Be quiet so you don't wake him up," Eva scolded quietly, the phone muffled again. I stilled when I heard her say that. "You know what will happen if you do."

"Eva, who's there that you don't want to wake up?" I asked.

"Her stupid husband."

"What? Why is he at your parents' house?"

"Because it's his night to take Jackson, and he was waiting for my sister to get home so she could get his stuff together."

"I don't think it's a good idea for her to be alone with him with everything happening," I warned. Eva had told me how Lucy's husband had physically assaulted her before she filed for divorce.

"I agree. That's why I'm here with her. But that's not why I called you," she said, changing the subject.

"Okay, why did you call?" I couldn't shake off the nagging feeling of worry about them being in the same house as Lucy's husband right now, but I knew fighting with her about it wouldn't help anything.

"Because I have evidence, and I need you to know the truth about the truth."

"Okay, what is the truth?"

"Kate and Cora—they don't like you. They aren't interested; they just want to screw you." She laughed hysterically, and I wondered if she was just fucking with me because she was still mad.

"So, they don't like me, but they want to screw me?" I asked, confused. "I guess that could be said about a lot of the women I've been with." I shrugged my shoulders, knowing that it was true.

"No, they want to *screw* you," she insisted.

My brows pinched together as I tried to figure out what she was trying to say.

"Son of a bitch!" she blurted out as I heard a crash in the background. I heard a commotion, followed by the sound of her running up the stairs.

"Eva—what's going on?!" I demanded, holding the phone tight against my ear.

"OPEN THIS DOOR NOW!" she screamed as another loud sound rang through the background. I could hear her fists pounding against the door.

"EVA!" I yelled, trying to get her to answer me. "What's going on?"

I rushed over to where my keys were lying by the mail on the kitchen counter and grabbed them. I had no idea where she was or what was going on. I just knew that I needed to get to her.

There was so much commotion, with voices yelling and everyone sounding panicked. My pulse raced as I tugged on my shoes and flew toward the door. Suddenly, there was a loud thud, and then the call ended.

"FUCK!" I shouted into my empty apartment and slammed my hand down on the counter.

Twenty-Eight
Ethan

My mom always said if I hadn't become a lawyer, then I should have become a detective. Apparently, I've always had this special knack for finding out information that I wasn't supposed to have. That knack was what led me to New York Presbyterian Hospital. I rushed to the emergency room lobby when I heard Eva's voice carrying through the empty hall.

"She's my sister! I need to be with her!" she cried hysterically.

"Ma'am, like I've already told you, she can't have anyone with her right now. The doctor will come out to give you an update when they have one."

I rounded the corner in time to wrap Eva in my arms as she turned to walk away. I looked her over as quickly as possible, searching her face when she looked up at me.

"Are you okay?" I asked with panic still rushing through me.

"Yes. I'm fine," she said and shook her head. "Lucy is in the emergency room. They won't let me back there with her."

"I'm sorry. I'm sure they'll have an update for you soon," I tried to reassure her as I led her away from the receptionist. "What the hell happened?"

We sat down in the empty chairs in the waiting area, and she folded her hands in her lap and looked down.

"I don't know." She shrugged, and a tear slid down her face. "There was a loud noise and yelling. I rushed upstairs as fast as I could, but the door was locked. By the time I got it open, she was unconscious on the floor."

"Did he hurt you?" I asked through clenched teeth. I was worried about Lucy, but I would also kill him if he laid a hand on Eva.

"No. I don't think so. I wasn't worried about me. I was just so focused on Lucy and making sure Jackson was okay."

"Eva!" A woman screamed and came running toward us. "What the hell happened?!"

"Lance went after Lucy. I tried to get in the room, but I couldn't. I couldn't stop him," she whispered, her voice shaky.

"What did the doctors say?"

"They won't let me back. They said that they'll update me, but who knows how long that will be," Eva said as her leg bounced anxiously. "You should have seen how pale she was in the ambulance. I've never been so scared before in my life."

I wrapped my arm tighter around Eva as the woman's eyes filled with tears. She blotted at them before seeming to notice me.

"Hi, I'm Ethan," I said, reaching over to shake the woman's hand. I assumed this was her other sister, given how much they looked like each other.

"Ethan?" she confirmed, looking from me to Eva with raised eyebrows. "As in…"

"As in, *the guy I work for*," Eva said through clenched teeth.

"Right…" She chuckled and shook my hand before giving Eva a dramatic wink. "I'm Gabi, Eva's other sister. The middle child, and therefore, obviously the coolest of the three of us."

I laughed and watched as Eva rolled her eyes.

"It's nice to meet you," I said, pulling my hand back as I caught the look Eva was giving her sister.

"Well, I think I'm going to go find coffee. Anyone want some?"

"No, thank you," I replied as Eva shook her head no.

Once we were alone again, I turned to face Eva and studied her face.

"Are you sure you're okay?" I asked, reaching over to rub her knee.

"Yeah. I'm just worried about my sister." She looked past me to the doors of the emergency room, looking to see if anyone would magically appear with an update.

"I know. I can only imagine how scared you are."

We sat there in silence for a few minutes as I tried to comfort her the best way that I could. Suddenly, she turned to me, and her eyes went wide as if she remembered something. She reached into her pocket and pulled out her cell phone, messing with the buttons before handing it to me.

"What I was calling to tell you earlier was that I found out something about Cora. Something I think you need to know." She pointed at the video that was paused on her phone and nodded.

I pressed play and waited for the video to start, my stomach already feeling in knots. Immediately, I noticed Kate sitting in a booth at a restaurant, laughing at something the other person had said. The camera moved slightly to the side, and I felt my blood pressure shoot through the roof as I saw Cora sitting next to her. No one else was in the video as they laughed and acted completely in love. When they leaned in for a kiss, I closed my eyes and pushed the phone away. I didn't need to see that bullshit.

"See, they're screwing you," Eva said, followed by a heavy sigh.

"Just because they're fucking doesn't mean that they're screwing me." I could feel the tension building in my shoulders.

"Think about it," Eva insisted, showing me the phone again. "Why would Cora want to have sex with you if she's into women? They want something from you. That's why they filed reports."

I worked my jaw back and forth as I thought about it. She had a point. Cora had made it abundantly clear that she didn't want a relationship with me. Just sex. Kate… Well, Kate wasn't anything I ever saw coming. I was completely thrown off when Regina pulled us in to talk to us about the complaint Kate had filed.

Someone walked out down the hallway, pulling our attention directly to them. I let out the breath I was holding when I saw that it was just the cleaning crew wheeling their supplies down the corridor. I wasn't in the mood to try to deal with the Kate and Cora bullshit that had just landed in my lap, so I decided to change the subject.

"So, I heard that we have a new employee starting on Monday," I said, hoping to lighten the mood, even though I knew it was near impossible given where we were and what had happened. The problem was that I didn't have any other good news to talk about.

"Are you mad that I didn't ask you before I recommended my sister for the job?" she asked nervously, chewing her nail.

"Honestly?" I asked, my eyebrows raised. I watched as the color drained from her face, and a look of worry washed over her beautiful face. "No, I'm not mad. I was a little blindsided by it, that's all."

She smiled, and her shoulders dropped as she relaxed a little.

"Do you think she'll be a good fit for our office?" I asked. While I didn't doubt that Eva was a good judge of character, I knew how easy it was for the lines to get blurred when you tried to have a professional relationship with your family. It took Garrett and me a few years before we were able to iron out that wrinkle at work.

"I really do," she said and nodded. "Lucy is the youngest, but she's also the most mature and independent. She's a natural-born leader, never breaks the rules, and genuinely cares about the job she does. Unfortunately, it's also been the reason that she's stayed with Lance for so long. But you can't blame her for wanting to try to make her marriage work when there is a child involved."

I smiled, knowing what kind of personality she was talking about. My mother stayed in a bad marriage for years because she thought it was what would be best for me and my brother. I wish I could go back in time and convince her that she was worth so much more than she ever gave herself credit for.

"Well, then, I'm happy to have her work for us."

"How did you hear about her getting the job anyway?" Eva asked, her brows pinched together.

"Regina called me before she brought her in for the interview. We discussed the struggle that she's had with finding a personal assistant for Luis. She was worried that it would take weeks, if not months, before she could find someone qualified to replace Kate. Moving her to Luis's department solved one problem but left her another. We agreed that if she felt like Lucy would be a good fit, she should go ahead and offer her the position. Obviously, we didn't need to check in with you since you had recommended her."

"Can I confess something?" She shifted in her seat, making sure she was still facing the doors to the emergency room.

"Sure," I said.

"I hate the idea that Kate is still going to be working there."

I sighed and pushed the air out forcefully.

"Yeah, me too. But it's not like we can fire her. She would immediately turn on us and come back with a wrongful termination lawsuit."

"How can she? New York is an At-Will state."

"You don't think she'll use the recent sexual harassment claim as proof that she was terminated as a means of retaliation?"

Eva paused for a moment and then shook her head.

"You're right. They would probably rule in her favor, too."

"Trust me, I hate it just as much as you do. But unless we had proof that she wasn't performing her job or violated one of the rules in the employee handbook, our hands are tied."

"You're right," she muttered as we saw Gabi heading back.

"Where's Jackson?" Gabi asked, sitting down beside Eva.

"He's with Mom and Dad. They had just got home when everything happened. Lance took off and left Jackson crying for him in the front yard without looking back. If only he knew what a real monster his dad was," Eva said, her hands starting to shake.

"Have you started a police report yet?" I asked, interrupting. My blood was boiling as my anger raged through me.

"I don't know if my parents have or not. I came in the ambulance with Lucy."

"I'll check in with Mom and see if they've had a chance to," Gabi offered, pulling her phone out of her back pocket.

"What's Lance's last name?" My voice was harder than usual, and the strain of getting the words out was evident.

"Why?" Eva asked at the same time her sister blurted out, "Conner."

"Thank you," I said with a warm smile as I pulled my cell phone out of my pocket. I was already dialing the number that I needed when I looked up and found Eva watching me. "Be sure to get some food in you and drink some water. I'll be back soon." I nodded to Eva as I turned and walked away, the phone pressed to my ear.

"Nate—I need a favor."

Twenty-Nine
Eva

It was after midnight when I checked my phone again, looking to see if I had a text message from Ethan. I had no idea where he went or what he was doing, but something told me that I wasn't going to like it when I found out. The monitors beeped steadily next to me as they confirmed that they were still working to keep my baby sister alive.

Lucy had been moved to the ICU and had yet to wake up. Her injuries were severe, with internal bleeding that required surgery. Her face was shades of blue and purple as the bruises started to set, along with the stitches across her cheek from where he split it open. My fingers were achy from holding her hand for so long in an awkward position, but I couldn't find the strength to let go.

My parents had found someone to watch Jackson as he slept, completely unaware that anything had happened. For now, he thought that his momma was working another graveyard shift at the hospital instead of worrying about how she was fighting for her life after his daddy tried to kill her. He was too little to have to worry about any of that, and we were determined to keep him from finding out if he didn't have to.

Brittany had been by my side while we were in the waiting room, but after Lucy was moved to the ICU, only one person was allowed to be with her. Even that was an exception the staff made for us, given how well they knew Lucy. I begged my family to go home and get some sleep, promising them that we would all take turns being with her until she woke up. There was no way that I was leaving her, and they all knew that.

My eyes felt heavy, desperate for sleep in the quiet, dark room. The margaritas had worn off the second I heard she was in trouble, but the after-effects were lingering pretty heavily. My body was sore and achy as I shifted my position in the uncomfortable chair beside her bed.

I was watching TV with the sound off when I heard my phone vibrate on the table next to me. I quickly slid my hand out of Lucy's and grabbed it before it could wake her up, which was silly, given how hard I was praying for her to wake up. I slid my finger across the screen to unlock it, relieved to find a text message from Ethan.

Ethan: Sorry, I got tied up. How's Lucy?

Me: She's been moved to the ICU but hasn't woken up. The surgery went well, but she's still fighting for her life.

I felt the tears slide down my face as I pressed send. How did the night turn so dramatically? We went from celebrating her new job and having a girls' night to me sitting in the hospital, praying she wouldn't die.

Ethan: Are you allowed to have company?

Me: No, they only allow one person in the room at a time—hospital rules.

Ethan: You know I don't follow the rules very well.

I rolled my eyes and felt guilty about the smile that was trying to spread across my face. Now wasn't the time or place to be smiling and feeling happy.

Me: So I've seen…

Ethan: I'm on my way up. What room is she in?

Me: They're not going to let you in. You have to have them unlock the door, and they're not going to. You should go home and get some rest. I'll text you an update tomorrow.

Ethan: What room?

He was persistent, to say the least. I was too exhausted to argue with him about this. He would have to find out on his own that they weren't going to let him up here.

Me: 1041

Ethan: On my way.

I put my phone down next to me and rubbed Lucy's hand before turning my attention back to the TV. A few minutes later, I heard the door open and expected to see a nurse coming in to check on Lucy. Ethan ducked his head in and smiled before slipping inside, holding the door as it gently closed. He gave me a quick head nod with a smile before he walked over and sat by me. I blinked a few times, convinced that I must have been so tired that I hallucinated that he was in the room.

"What are you doing here?" I hissed quietly at him.

"I told you I was on my way up." He shrugged as he quietly pulled the other chair over and sat beside me.

"Did you sneak up here? You're going to get in trouble, and they're going to kick you out…"

"They let me in," he said as he leaned back and rested his ankle on his knee. "How are you holding up?"

I sighed heavily, feeling the weight of the world on my shoulders.

"I'm tired." I leaned back to relax when the light hit his face, and I saw the outline of a black eye. "What the hell happened to you?!" I asked in a harsh whisper.

"It's nothing." He shook his head and looked away.

"Ethan..."

"I took care of the problem, okay?"

"No. Not okay." I blew out a heavy breath and gently let go of Lucy's hand as anger rushed through me.

"We need to talk. Now." I stood up and walked over to the corner of the room. It was far away enough from Lucy's bed that we wouldn't disturb her, but it was close enough that I could still see her.

I waited impatiently as Ethan stood up and followed me over. He shoved his hands in his pockets and leaned against the counter behind him. His head was lowered as if he were afraid to look at me.

"What did you do?" I asked again, my arms folded over my chest.

"I went to visit Lance. It just took a little longer to find him than I'd thought."

"How did you even know where to look? All you had was his name."

"I have a friend who owed me a favor," he said and looked away.

"What kind of favor?" I asked, raising my eyebrow.

"Does it matter?" he responded, raising his eyebrow in return.

"You bet your ass it does," I said with exasperation. "I need to know what happened so I can protect my sister!"

"Trust me—Lance won't put a hand on your sister ever again. I can promise you that."

"Would you please just stop being difficult and tell me what happened?" I was starting to lose my patience and sanity, all at the same time.

"Eva, you don't need to know the details. Okay? The less I say, the better."

"You're really starting to worry me. Is Lance dead?"

"No."

"Then how do you know that he won't come after her again?" I asked.

"Because I promised him that if he ever laid a hand on her again, I would be the one to dig the hole that his body would be thrown in."

"You *threatened* him?" My eyes were wide with shock.

"No. A threat is something you say but don't mean it. I meant every word of what I said." He pushed off from the counter and went to sit down.

I wasn't done with the conversation and had a thousand questions for him. As I marched back over to where he was, I stopped dead in my tracks when I saw Lucy's eyes flicker open.

Thirty
Ethan

My jaw was sore from the one spot where Lance had landed a punch before I took him down. He was a typical douchebag—good at running his mouth and beating up women but couldn't hold his own in a fight against a real man to save his life. Nate had confirmed where I would be able to find him and gave me the name of the woman he was screwing around with, which made it that much easier to get him where I wanted him.

After a few blows to the head, I had finally knocked some common sense into him. Or, more so, informing him to stay the fuck away from Lucy and to drop the custody case. I also reminded him that he was a fucking loser who wasn't worthy of Lucy and that he would give her whatever she wanted in the divorce. When I mentioned my *friend* Timothy, who happened to be the husband of the secretary he was fucking, he suddenly agreed to whatever I demanded.

I wasn't necessarily proud of what I had done, but I couldn't look the other way when my childhood was staring me in the fucking face. Some men didn't deserve to get whatever they wanted simply because they could buy their way to it, and I was happy to deliver that message to him.

Eva had been at Lucy's side throughout the night

and into the morning, never leaving other than for a quick bathroom break when she felt her bladder might burst. I had offered to bring her coffee and something for breakfast. She declined, not wanting to eat in front of her sister until she had been cleared to have solid foods again.

The doctors and nurses had been bustling through her room since she woke up, running different tests and tracking her vitals. It had been a relief to hear that she appeared to be doing better than they had expected, and the doctor felt confident she would have a quick recovery. They had a few more tests that they were waiting on before they would decide whether to release her or keep her for another night.

"How's your pain?" Eva asked, gently fluffing the pillow behind Lucy's head. "Do you want me to get the nurse?"

"I'm fine." She laughed, her voice hoarse. "Stop fussing over me. I gave birth without pain meds. I can manage this, too."

"Childbirth is different than recovering from surgery after your husband beat the shit out of you," Eva muttered quietly. Lucy looked up at her and gave her a sad smile.

"I'm sorry," Eva said. "I just really hate him and wish that you didn't have to go through this."

"I know. Me too." Lucy sighed. "But I meet with Art on Monday, and then we're supposed to have the mediation. Maybe things will be peaceful for once."

I felt Eva's eyes pierce me from across the room and looked away. I turned my attention to the TV and pretended to be watching the cooking show that was on.

"What's that about?" Lucy asked, pointing back and forth between Eva and me.

Eva looked at me and shrugged, forcing Lucy's attention to me.

"Well?" She narrowed her eyes and gave me the *mom* look.

"You'll have to get the details from Eva, but let's just say that Lance and I talked. You won't be seeing or hearing from him. And if you do, you just let me know." I smiled smugly and turned back to the TV.

"What details?" Lucy asked Eva.

"I've yet to hear them," Eva said through gritted teeth. "He hasn't said much about what happened."

"Exactly. And that's how it's gonna stay." I laughed softly and stood up. "I'm gonna head home and clean up. Do you need anything before I go?" I looked at Eva and watched as she blushed in front of her sister.

"No, thank you. I think we're good," she said and gently squeezed Lucy's shoulder.

"Okay, call me if you change your mind." I lowered my eyes from Eva to Lucy. "Lucy, I'm glad to see you're feeling better. Please let me know if you need anything as well."

"Thank you," she said sweetly.

I wanted to stay and talk to Eva, to make sure that Lucy really was okay, but I knew it was better if I left. Especially since I could tell how much it was bothering Eva that I wouldn't tell her what happened with Lance. The less she knew, the better.

Thirty-One
Eva
Two Weeks Later

"Do you think she's okay?" I asked Ethan, glancing down at my watch. She had been in the boardroom with Art for over an hour after he agreed to come here instead of having her go to his office. The original meeting had been postponed due to Lucy's recovery in the hospital. Ethan had explained the last-minute request and threw in lunch to get Art to agree. He might have been the best family law lawyer in Manhattan, but he was also a crotchety old man with a weakness for fried chicken.

"She's fine," he replied softly and sat down on the edge of my desk. "You have to stop worrying about her."

"She's my baby—"

"Sister. Yes, I know."

I blew out a slow, heavy breath and leaned back against my chair. Images of Lucy in the hospital, fighting for her life, continued to haunt me. I was thankful that she had the best team of doctors and nurses to care for her. On top of that, her boss finally took the stick out of her ass and helped Lucy by paying out her unused vacation and sick time, along with setting up a fund to help Lucy and Jackson get on their feet with Lucy starting a new job. My parents had more or less forced Lucy and Jackson to stay with them for a minimum of six months, which had really put my mind at ease.

It was a busy Monday, but I could not get myself to focus on anything other than Lucy's first day at Roberts and Associates or the fact that she was meeting with Art regarding some last-minute *change* to the custody case. My stomach was in knots as I sat there waiting for an update.

"Okay," I said, conceding, "Tell me something to distract me. Anything."

He leaned back, and a mischievous smile split his cheeks.

"You taste like honeydew."

I felt my cheeks flush as I looked up at him under my lashes.

"Well, that is definitely distracting," I admitted.

"You're telling me." He chuckled. "I'm sitting here, knowing that you're wearing that short-ass skirt, thinking about how I could climb under your desk and eat that sweet pussy without anyone knowing."

"That does sound very tempting." I giggled. "But I think we're going to have to make office sex off-limits now that my sister works here."

"In all honestly, we probably should have called it off-limits from the start." He laughed.

I heard footsteps coming down the hall and leaned forward, hoping it was Lucy. Regina turned and walked into my office, crumbling my hopes as she came in.

"Don't be so excited to see me," she said playfully,

noticing my reaction.

"I'm sorry. I thought you were Lucy."

Regina peeked her head out into the hallway, checking her desk.

"Is she still meeting with that lawyer?" she asked.

"Yeah. I was hoping they would be done by now." I reached up and moved my hair over my shoulder. "What's up?"

"Well, speaking of lawyers," she said cheerfully, "I've spoken to ours about the sexual harassment claims against Ethan." She closed the door and sat down after Ethan scooted off the desk and stood behind me.

"What's the news?" Ethan asked, folding his arms over his chest. I could smell the intoxicating scent of his cologne behind me.

"After some digging on Friday, our IT department was able to get some more information about the printed chat messages." Regina paused for a minute and shuffled through the stack of papers in her hand. "It turns out that Kate wasn't lying about the network glitch, and some of her reports had been printed in Eva's office. However, it's such a weird coincidence that it would happen at the same time Eva stepped away and left her computer unlocked. It feels as though Kate planned it, and that's what we're looking into now. I have no idea how she knew that you guys were chatting about that. But it was the perfect setup, to say the least."

She stopped to grab a piece of paper out of the pile and laid it on the desk in front of us. It was a printout of the sexual harassment claim Cora had filed at Hyde and Wilson before she filed the actual lawsuit.

"After Ethan sent me the video and pictures of Kate

and Cora together, I forwarded them to our legal department. Combined with the information that Ethan had given us about the other lawsuit she filed with Hyde and Wilson, we are trying to find a motive behind it. It seems as though she narrowed it down to two very successful lawyers from whom she felt she could get the biggest payout, but we don't have proof of that just yet. Our IT department is going through Kate's emails now, and they're recovering Cora's from when she was employed here. I'll keep you updated on what we find," Regina said as she gathered the paper from the desk and stood up.

"Thank you," Ethan said with a nod as Regina opened the door and left.

I felt some relief after she left, knowing that they were looking into finding the same missing piece that I had been stressing over before everything had happened with Lucy. Was that all on the same day? At this point, it felt like the days were blending.

"How are you doing?" Ethan asked as he moved behind me and gently rubbed my shoulders.

"It's been a long week, but I'm hoping that things will be resolved soon. It would be nice to be able to go back to some sort of normal."

I had my eyes closed while I enjoyed the feel of his hands on my skin as the stress melted away.

"Am I interrupting?" Lucy asked as she knocked lightly on the door. She looked happy, which I prayed was a good sign that things had gone well in her meeting with Art.

"Not at all," I said happily. "How did it go?"

She smiled as she walked in and sat down gently in front of me. I saw her wince and immediately felt concerned that she was already pushing herself too hard.

"I'm fine—" she interrupted before I could speak. "Just a little sore. That's all."

I let out a heavy breath and tried to force myself to relax.

"So…" I coaxed.

"Art brought me the new paperwork that was sent over to him early this morning from Jeremy's office. Lance has agreed to allow me full custody, and he's not fighting me on the items we were supposed to go to mediation over. I'm also going to file a restraining order for Jackson and me."

She stopped for a moment, and a peaceful smile spread across her face.

"I'm getting everything that I asked for."

I could feel my heart pounding as I was overjoyed by the news. The happiness on her face was contagious as my smile spread across my face.

"Lucy, I'm so happy to hear that," I said softly. "I knew everything would work out perfectly for you."

"Just like how things are working out perfectly for you, too," Lucy offered, looking between us before she got up and walked out, closing the door behind her.

I blushed, wondering what Ethan must be thinking. While Ethan and I had said we loved each other, we hadn't talked about when we would start telling people we were together. Aside from Regina, we hadn't talked much about our new relationship, especially with everything else that had happened.

When I looked up to try to explain, I found him staring at me with a devilish grin.

"What's that grin about?" I asked curiously.

"Stop overthinking it," he said smugly.

"Overthinking what?"

"Whether I think your sister thinks we're in a relationship."

"How did you know?" I whispered.

"I can read you like a book," he joked.

"Oh yeah? Then what am I thinking now?" I asked as my stomach grumbled quietly.

"That you want to burn some toast for breakfast." He raised a brow and started laughing when my face confirmed that he was right.

Thirty-Two
Ethan
Two Months Later

Even though I was a lawyer, I hated being in the courtroom. My foot tapped on the tile floor beneath me as I sat waiting for the verdict in this bullshit sexual harassment case against me. I looked over my shoulder and felt calmer when I saw Eva sitting next to Regina, smiling at me.

The judge entered the courtroom, and everyone rose before being informed we could be seated. The chairs shuffled against the floors of the quiet room, the sound of time ticking by at an irritatingly slow pace. Finally, the judge cleared his throat and began. I tuned everything out until he got to the sentence that I had been needing to hear.

My ears perked up, and I swear a chorus of angels sang in the back row when he announced that the case was being dismissed due to lack of evidence. I closed my eyes and pulled in a deep breath, feeling relieved that something had finally started to go right.

As the room cleared out, I noticed that Kate was still sitting in the back of the room, tears staining her face. Cora had stormed out as soon as she was able to, and I just assumed that Kate had gone with her.

I stood up and straightened my tie before walking over to where Eva and Regina were standing, waiting for me. Garrett was off in the corner, talking with one of the lawyers from Hyde and Wilson. They had shown up to support our office after their lawsuit was dismissed, giving us high hopes for the same result.

"Congratulations," Eva squealed, wrapping her arms around me before planting a gentle kiss on my lips.

"Thank you, baby. I'm glad that it was dismissed."

"Me too," Regina piped in, smiling from ear to ear.

I looked past her to see Kate approaching us, her head tucked in shame.

"Can I talk to you for a minute?" she asked quietly.

"I don't think that's the best idea," I said sternly, placing my hand on Eva's lower back to guide her away.

"Please—I know that I messed up, and I just want the opportunity to explain what happened," Kate insisted.

"I think we're long past that," Eva muttered under her breath. Kate looked at her and lowered her eyes.

"I'm sorry for what I did. I really am," she said shakily. "I didn't mean for things to go this far. I never meant for you to get hurt."

I put my hand up to stop her.

"This sounds like an admission of some sort. You really need to stop and consider whether or not you should be speaking about this without legal counsel," I warned. Not that I owed her anything. I just didn't have it in me to worry about another fucking scandalous lawsuit.

"I'm fully aware of that, but I need to say this," Kate continued. "I didn't know that things would escalate this far.

If I would've known, I wouldn't have gone through with it."
She pulled in a deep breath and looked between us.

"Cora and I have been dating for a few years. We decided last year that we wanted to have a baby. You can probably understand how complicated that is for two women unless you have the money to do it the right way. Well, after several failed rounds of IVF with me, we didn't have the money to spend for Cora to try. She was working for another attorney, and he was insistent on helping. It was a terrible idea, but he offered his services, and she agreed. They'd had sex, and she hoped that she would get pregnant. While it wasn't how we wanted to do it, in the end, we would have a baby. That was all that mattered at the time."

She rubbed her hands down the front of her jeans and looked over her shoulder to see if anyone was listening.

"Well, after they had sex, Cora didn't want to do it again. But he became obsessed. He would constantly try to touch her, and it got so uncomfortable that she filed a complaint. Human Resources moved her to another department and brushed it under the carpet without bothering to look into it. So, she quit and got a job with Roberts and Associates. After she started working with us, she overheard someone talking about a sexual harassment lawsuit where the woman won thousands of dollars because the attorney didn't want his wife to find out. That's when Cora decided to file the lawsuit against the other attorney."

I could feel my blood pressure rise as I listened, knowing where this was going.

"But then something happened. Something changed," Kate said and shook her head in shame. "Cora became so obsessed with the idea of a quick and easy payout that she went after you next. I didn't know that she had sex with you until after it had happened. And if I'm being honest, it almost broke us. She apologized, and then we found out she was pregnant. I was so excited about that baby that I just figured it had been a rough patch we had to work through.

"We were having a baby, and that's what we wanted. Then she filed the lawsuit against you, and I couldn't believe it. I asked her to undo it, but she wouldn't. She was adamant that if she could win the two cases, then we would have enough money never to have to worry about anything again. I told her that it was wrong, that she had already gotten what she wanted. That *we* were getting what we wanted. A baby."

Tears started to fall down her face as she wiped them away with the back of her hand.

"Cora was getting frustrated because she wasn't getting anywhere with the other lawsuit. Her lawyer was dragging his feet, which is what happens when you find the cheapest, shadiest lawyer out there. She convinced me to file a claim that you had sexually harassed me as well." She lowered her eyes, unable to look at me. "I told her that I couldn't do that because we were never around each other. But really, I just couldn't do it to you."

"But you did," I bit out angrily.

"I know." She nodded her head. "I felt like my life was crumbling beneath me. When I walked into Eva's office to grab my reports from the printer, I saw the chat up on her computer. It was a terrible moment of weakness and complete and utter stupidity on my part, but I was desperate. I printed them and held them in my drawer until I could find the strength to get rid of them."

"And again, you didn't," Eva said, narrowing her eyes at Kate.

"I am so, very sorry. I could apologize every day for the rest of my life, and it would never be enough. I understand that. And I'm sorry for everything that Cora has put you through. If it makes you feel any better, we've broken up. She's now having a baby with an attorney who won't leave her alone now that he knows she's carrying his baby."

"He got a paternity test?" I asked, needing confirmation that there was no way this child was mine.

I felt Eva's hand squeeze mine. I knew that it was odd to have a paternity test done while the mother was still pregnant, but I didn't care enough about this to inquire why they had decided to do it. Maybe there was another reason for doing the procedure, or maybe Cora was just pushed that far into a corner with the other lawsuit. Who the fuck knew at this point?

"Results were conclusive that he is the biological father," Kate said as she reached out and handed me an envelope.

I took it from her and pulled out a copy of the paternity test.

"Again, I'm really sorry for everything that happened. I know that it doesn't change anything, but at least now you know why I did it. I was young, stupid, and in love. But that doesn't excuse me or my behavior."

Kate lowered her head and walked away. It felt good to know the truth, but hell if it didn't bother me how much was happening without me knowing.

"I'm gonna go and give you two a few minutes alone," Regina said, gently touching my arm before walking over to where Garrett was.

Eva looked up at me and studied my face.

"So, how are you feeling now?" she asked.

"It's been a lot to take in. But I'm glad things are all falling into place, and the shitty parts are over. Now, I can focus on being happy and eating burnt toast with my girlfriend," I said with a smile.

"Girlfriend?" she asked, her voice going up an octave.

"If you'll have me…" I said shyly, bending down to kiss her forehead.

"As long as you promise to make me toast and peanut butter smores," she replied as she wrapped her arms around my neck.

"Deal." I leaned in for a kiss, savoring this moment for as long as I could.

****

Thank you so much for reading Breaking All The Rules! I hope you enjoyed it!

If you'd like to hang out and talk books, find me on Facebook in my reader group, Samantha Baca's Smutties! We'd love to have you!!
https://www.facebook.com/groups/2945710968775398/

If you're looking for your next great read, be sure to check out my full list of books on the next page! I love to dabble in everything, so you'll find plenty of steamy romantic suspense, as well as witty, spicy romantic comedies and holiday novellas!

Other Books By Samantha Baca

The Haven Brook Series
(small-town romantic suspense)

'Til Death Do Us Part (Haven Brook Book 1)
https://books2read.com/u/m2RJNR

The Cradle Will Fall (Haven Brook Book 2)
https://books2read.com/u/b6O0QE

The Ties That Bind (Haven Brook Book 3)
https://books2read.com/u/mqgoz8

A Very Haven Christmas (Haven Brook Book 4- Novella)
https://books2read.com/u/mvqGjj

Three Strikes, You're Gone (Haven Brook Book 5)
https://books2read.com/u/mvqL2z

The Dark Shadows Trilogy
(romantic suspense)

Five Steps Ahead (Dark Shadows Book 1)
https://books2read.com/u/38Q0gO

Ten Seconds Too Late (Dark Shadows Book 2)
https://books2read.com/u/3JRgVB

Against The Clock (Dark Shadows Book 3)
https://books2read.com/u/m2YwoR

<u>Beaumont Creek Series</u>
<u>(small town)</u>
Just One Time (Beaumont Creek Book 1)
https://books2read.com/u/3G52zK

Second Chances (Beaumont Creek Book 2)
https://books2read.com/u/4Aj6Z0

Third Time's The Charm (Beaumont Creek Book 3)
https://books2read.com/u/b5lEyG

Four-ever Single (Beaumont Creek Book 4)
https://books2read.com/u/4j5jMX

Fifth Wheel (Beaumont Creek Book 5)
https://books2read.com/u/4XwKwa

<u>Whiskey Mountain Series</u>
<u>(small-town- novellas)</u>
Something To Talk About
https://books2read.com/u/4X62ag

Something To Think About
https://books2read.com/u/3GWAan

Something To Believe In
https://books2read.com/u/3yVzgB

Something To Live For
https://books2read.com/u/mllEOP

<u>Sugarplum Falls Series</u>
<u>(Holiday Novellas- can be read as standalone)</u>

Blame It On The Mistletoe
https://books2read.com/u/bw1rqe

Blame It On The Eggnog
https://books2read.com/u/38PPY6

Blame It On The Candy Canes
https://books2read.com/u/31DNo7

Blame It On The Blizzard
https://books2read.com/u/b6z6XE

Blame It On The Reindeer
https://books2read.com/u/baLAG6

Blame It On The Carols
https://books2read.com/u/me8E9z

Blame It On The Lattes
https://books2read.com/u/mB1E2A

Blame It On The Secret Santa
https://books2read.com/u/mY9dGY

Blame It On The Holidays: A collection of bonus epilogues
https://books2read.com/u/bwXRPY

<u>The Stone Creek Series</u>
<u>(small-town- novellas)</u>
Chocolate Covered Mistletoe (Stone Creek Book 1)
https://books2read.com/u/3LRk9N

Candy Coated Promises (Stone Creek Book 2)
https://books2read.com/u/mldP5Y

Pumpkin Spiced Possibilities (Stone Creek Book 3)
https://books2read.com/u/bojdwV

<u>Standalone Books</u>
One Last Wish
https://books2read.com/u/mqg7D9

Finding Love In Apartment 2C (novella)
https://books2read.com/u/bze9aZ

Breaking All The Rules
(Previously published as: Cocky Counsel:
A Hero Club Novel)
https://books2read.com/u/box2MZ

All Is Fair In Food And War (novella)
https://books2read.com/u/bp8qjX

Holiday Books
(novellas)

Snow Place To Go
https://books2read.com/u/4A560N

A Very Merry Kissmas
https://books2read.com/u/bPDgy7

A Christmas Wish
https://books2read.com/u/4EKXpE

Holiday Hijinks
https://books2read.com/u/4DP6Ze

Acknowledgments

It's always a wonderful feeling when I finish a book, but this one was different because it was changing a book I had already written. When I first got invited to write in the Cocky Hero Club world, I was beyond excited! It was such a dream come true! And I will forever be grateful for that opportunity. However, several years later—and 30+ books later—my writing changed drastically, and I knew that this book deserved a new life.

I'm so thankful to my alpha readers, Azucena, Claire, Tamara, and Valerie, for their help with working through this book and all of the changes it went through. I appreciate the time and effort you ladies put into making this book better! Thank you for always being a bright light in the book world—as well as mine. You're the best!

I'd also like to thank my beta readers, Jackie, Karrie, and Malissa, for taking this on once I finished allllll of the editing and had something worth reading. I value your feedback and love your excitement every time I have a new book, even if you've read it before! Thank you so much for all of your help!

My family has and always will be my greatest support. I love and adore their enthusiasm every time I talk about a new book or when something exciting happens in my author life. I never have to wonder who is in my corner because I know it will always be them. Thank you for always believing in me and for encouraging me to chase after my dreams. Mom, Dad, Sarah, Richard, and my girls—I love you guys so much!!

This dream of being a writer wouldn't be possible without the constant love and support of my husband. Thank you for being the biggest Dick a girl could ever ask for and for showing up every single time I need you. We make a great team, baby. Thank you for always believing in me and for not panicking every time I said, "So, I did a thing…".

My sweet girls—I will never stop being proud to be your mother, and I hope that when you're older, you'll see what I did and go after your dreams. I will always be by your side to help you along the way. Dream big, my loves!

And as always, thank you so much to my readers. I don't think there will ever be a time when I'm not humbled by how many people read my books or when someone comes up to me at an event and says that I'm one of their favorite authors. Thank you so much! I am the luckiest author in the world to have such amazing readers!!!

About the Author

Samantha lives in the southwest with her husband and two children, where she enjoys writing, drinking iced coffee, and watching the greatest show of all time—Friends. With over 30 books published, Samantha enjoys writing across several different genres, from steamy romantic suspense to laugh-out-loud spicy romantic comedies. She also has a sweet spot for holiday stories, so grab a blanket and get ready to binge some of the sweetest—yet spicy—holiday romance your heart can handle!

Samantha loves connecting with her readers, so here's a list of where you can find her:

Facebook Reader Group:
https://www.facebook.com/groups/2945710968775398/

Facebook:
https://www.facebook.com/AuthorSamanthaBaca

Instagram:
https://instagram.com/author_samantha_baca

Webpage:
www.samanthabaca.com

Goodreads:
http://www.goodreads.com/authorsamanthabaca

Books2Read:
https://books2read.com/ap/RQAYK9/Samantha-Baca